Sophie

Jennifer Dawson was brought up in south London and educated at St Annes's College, Oxford, and University College, London. She has worked as a teacher, a social worker in a psychiatric hospital, a welfare worker in London's East End, an indexer, a sub-editor and on the Supplement to the Oxford English Dictionary. She loves France and her other interests include music, the countryside, London and the Spanish Civil War. She has published four previous novels: *The Ha-Ha*, which won the James Tait Black Award in 1962 and was later televised, *Fowler's Snare*, which won the Cheltenham Festival Award in 1963, *The Cold Country* and *Strawberry Boy*. With Elizabeth Mitchell she wrote a children's book, *The Queen of Trent*. She now lives in Oxford.

ALSO BY JENNIFER DAWSON

The Ha-Ha
Fowler's Snare
The Cold Country
Strawberry Boy
The Queen of Trent (with Elizabeth Mitchell)

HOSPITAL WEDDING

Stories by Jennifer Dawson

QUARTET BOOKS
LONDON MELBOURNE NEW YORK

First published by Quartet Books Limited 1978
A member of the Namara Group
27 Goodge Street, London W1P 1FD

This book has been published with financial assistance from the Arts Council of Great Britain

ISBN 0 7043 2176 9

Typeset by Bedford Typesetters Limited
Printed in Great Britain by litho at The Anchor Press Ltd
and bound by Wm Brendon & Son Ltd
both of Tiptree, Essex

THE BLEEDING HEARTS

'So Reg decided to take a big salary-cut.' Flora hadn't meant to boast. 'And we left Rhodesia.' The black girl merely stared out of the window though and wrapped her hands round her mug of coffee and shivered.

'Do please come nearer the fire,' Flora turned another bar on. The black girl came closer and stared out at the black sky against the window, and the office workers huddled very still against the bus stop opposite, and the rush-hour traffic jam.

'So in spite of this ghastly English climate,' Flora looked for her visitor's face, 'in spite of it all, we're still glad we came away. A white man can't hold up his head in Africa these days.'

'Oh?' The black girl frowned slightly and swallowed her coffee and gave a slight yawn: 'I see' she said politely, fumbling in her bag.

'Do please come nearer the fire.'

It was a freezing November and even the pigeons that usually paced backwards and forwards in twos and threes along the window-sills had given up movement and squashed themselves against the chimney-pots outside the windows to keep warm.

Flora had seen the black girl standing on the stairs when she left the block that morning for the school where she taught. She had seen her standing there outside Number Ten waiting patiently, and she was still standing there when she got back that evening – still leaning over the rusty iron bannisters and yawning. The evening fog of traffic exhaust that seeped up the stairwell and between the fancy ironwork ferns up the bannisters had stained her white fur coat, and she was wiping it very slowly and sighing:

'Oh dear!'

Flora could hear her sighs before she saw her there. They followed her up the shushing mica steps and echoed round the stairwell as she fumbled for her keys and let herself into her flat.

'Won't you come in and keep yourself warm till your friend gets back?' she leaned over and called down, and her voice ran round the stone well.

'Oh?' The girl stared up doubtfully, then she agreed, and slowly came up dragging a large canvas-covered box. 'Thank you,' she put her frozen hands round her mug of coffee.

'Do you live in this neighbourhood?'

'Uh?'

'Do you – ' but a lorry passing in the street below blocked off the rest, and when it had gone, the high shrill of a burglar-alarm started off: 'Oh dear. That noise will go on all week-end now. They go home at five in that shop. Sometimes it rings for three days.'

'Uh?'

'Do you work round here?' But the visitor was listening for front doors to open and fumbling in her bag.

'So we took the salary cut and said goodbye to our friends. It just wasn't possible to operate as a human being out there any more.'

'Yes, I see,' she went through some papers in her bag and turned the collar of her coat up. Her teeth were chattering. She said her name was Sede.

Flora didn't like to ask her where she came from in case she was British, so she asked again: 'What do you do?' staring at the big cardboard box at Sede's side.

'I'm a nurse,' she wound her watch. 'Can you please tell me something?'

'Surely. Go ahead.'

'Can you tell me where I can find a hotel or a clean boarding house round here for one night only? In case he doesn't come back till tomorrow morning,' she gestured to the public stair. 'This clock is very heavy to carry round and round,' she put her foot on the parcel. Her voice was low and broken.

'There's a place called "Welsh Grove" just up the road on the right. Leave the clock here if you like while you go up and see if they have a room.'

'I see,' Sede stared round. Then she was gone. The clock gave a loud stinging chime.

An hour later Sede stood there again in her street-fouled coat. A motorist had driven a puddle over it and cigarette stubs from the corners of the public stair had been spat down by the wind that blew through the block, and clung in its fur.

'Success?' Flora asked.

'They wanted three pounds down' Sede said softly.

'I'm sure that's not normal.'

'Oh?' A faint whistling came from Sede's throat, and for the first time Flora stared into her big sad eyes.

'Still, I daresay your friend will be back by now,' she opened the door.

'My friend?' Sede frowned.

'From downstairs at Number Ten.'

'Oh no. He's my landlord. He took my month's rent and then bolted the door and put my stuff outside.' She gently put her toe on the clock.

'Did you go to the police?'

'Oh yes, but they said come round here and sort it out with him.'

They went down to Number Ten together, but the flat was in darkness. No one knew who lived there. 'We won't put up with that kind of thing,' Flora said. 'You write a note from our address and put it through, and Reg will go and see him when he gets in tonight. In the meantime, make yourself at home.'

'Oh?' Sede stared at Flora's sitting room and sat down again gingerly on the edge of the chair and huddled there in her coat, drawing her thin lips inwards against her teeth. 'Thank you.'

'You'd better stay the night! Then you'll be sure to catch him.'

'Thank you. Which is my room?' She had just showed Sede the divan in her husband's small workroom when the telephone went. Flora took the receiver up with some triumph. It would be Reg and he'd be delighted with their first black guest in a multi-racial country. But the call was for Sede, and she lifted the whole phone up bodily in her fur coat and carried it into the workroom and shut the door. The clock chimed again. Sede had only been here an hour, and she was already in the phone book, apparently.

'How did they know our number?' Flora asked when Sede came out.

'It was a wrong number.' Flora stared. 'Or it was that hotel.' But before Flora could say:

'Well make up your mind,' the front-door bell went. It wasn't the landlord from Number Ten, but two tall thin black men carrying a TV set, a large bundle in a sheet, and a statue of a Victorian soldier standing at attention with a woggly head.

'Mind that head!' Sede cried, then: 'Oh Christ, they brought it all! These stupid small island people. I told them just to bring the key of the clock. And they brought it all!'

When Reg came in that night Flora was airing sheets and Sede was standing at the window clasping a cup of hot water and sprinkling handfuls of tea on and sniffing and sneezing and shivering. The little workroom was transformed. There was a brown cloth on the table and a conch shell full of scented ink. Two oleographs called 'Breaking the Ice' and 'The Girls Find the Swans' Home' hung on the wall, and the two men had fixed the TV set on top of a pile of the art books and were watching a programme about dolphins eating ice-cream. They all stood there. The dolphins put their heads in plastic bags with pictures of Berkshire villages stamped on them. Then the weatherman gave tomorrow's forecast.

'Please make yourself at home,' Flora smiled round the room. 'I'll make some tea.' Her husband came after her. She told him about the landlord at Number Ten.

'There were frozen tears on her cheeks. All day! Just standing there.' She heard Reg go back; heard someone say what a fine city Nottingham was:

'The times we had there' they were laughing. 'Have you ever been to Nottingham?' they asked Reg.

'No. I really must go there some time,' he sat on the edge of his chair fidgeting with the keys in his pockets. He came out to the kitchen and fidgeted one accidentally into a cup of tea and splashed his face and suit.

'Never mind,' Flora cried as he wiped the stains, 'you might have got those splashes fighting in the Spanish Civil War.'

'Now now. Don't start putting ideas into my head' he tried to laugh the remark off.

The flat was silent though when the Peets got up next morning. They were having their breakfast when Sede came in dressed to go out.

'Off already? Why not have some breakfast first?'

'Oh no thank you.' She took some boiling water and sprinkled tea on and sipped.

'What time do you have to be on duty? Which hospital is it?'

'I felt obliged to leave there because those nurses think only of getting into bed with men. So I am studying to be a district nurse only I've got to pass my driver's tests first and that man at the driving school said I must pay him for thirty lessons first – and the insurance, before I can begin to learn. Is this normal?'

'Certainly not.'

'So I took the punched card operators' course, but when I get there, they say they are full up.'

'The bloody so-and-so's!' Reg said politely reading his newspaper.

'Racists!' Flora cried.

'What time will you be coming to collect your stuff tonight, Sede, so that one of us can be in?'

'What time will be convenient?' she asked softly. 'Reg – please – you have been so good to me. You say what time. Or maybe I will sit on the doorstep again when I get back from my Receipts Ledger Clerk interview. I will stand by the bannisters and wait till you are home.'

'Oh dear no!' Flora protested. 'We wouldn't allow that again. Reg will drive your stuff round, won't you, Reg? When he's had it out with your landlord at Number Ten.'

'Thank you, Reg,' Sede lifted her long thin face gratefully from her tea.

'Where to, Sede?'

'Which left-luggage office would you recommend? Some of those metal lockers at the station are too small for one TV set, two pix, the statue . . . Which station would you advise, Reg?'

'I'll go down to Number Ten now and see what's going on.'

The postman was standing outside Number Ten:

'That was a fly-by-night if you ask me . . . Took rents from coloured people for places he didn't own. But he's been gone for weeks now.'

'Sede, I'm afraid your landlord was a bad egg. A no-gooder.'

'Oh? I see.'

'A racist' Flora added.

'I see.' So Sede became their golden opportunity to atone for their country.

'You must stay till you've found somewhere permanent. We won't charge you till you get your job. But perhaps we should ask for a reference, Sede. It's normal procedure.'

'I see. I'll ask Bishop Corbey to write me one today. What time will you be home so that I know when to get it by?'

'Oh early. I'm a teacher and I only get playground duty once or twice a week.'

'Yes, but what time?' Sede gave a patient whistling noise in her throat and half shut her eyes. She looked very tired.

'About four. But here's the spare key just in case. Good luck for the job-hunt.'

The flat was very quiet when Flora got in from school that afternoon. Sede was lying on the divan reading *Woman's Realm* and cutting her toenails. She had hung some thick velour curtains at the window and spread a tartan plastic cover over the bed. Another picture – the Queen and the Duke of Edinburgh on a montage of Edinburgh – hung with the others on the wall.

'How cosy you've made the room. Did you get the job?'

'They were racists at the Receipts Ledger Clerk Office. I think' Sede whispered, looking at Flora. 'I think.'

The 'vertical street' is said to be lonely. But the Peets never had a dull moment now. The staircase was a narrow spiral with three front doors to each dark breathing-space placed so that every transaction at each one was heard down the length of the stone funnel. The street windows of the block couldn't be opened because of the traffic noise and filth, so the tenants would put their front doors on chains for ventilation and for the view of everyone who went up or down. Most of them were elderly and had a whole day to lean on their chains. At Number One a retired ship's steward with a surgical leg would put his stick out as Flora passed:

'Are you all right up there alone with them? Knock me up if you want a hand.' Or the ex-school-teacher at Number Three would see her and call out anxiously:

'There was a wounded bird crying piteously on the ledge under your window, so I went up while you were out. Just to see if there was anything I could do to relieve its pain. You are brave to have so many people staying with you. Where is their real home?' Or the Pakistani electrician would put his eye to the spy-glass in his door and bob out:

'I have succeeded in fixing it for you. It was a very serious fuse and they could have had serious trouble and bad shock. And I do not want those Africans in your flat should think that they can plug any plug into any wall and chant a spell over it. I am obliged to charge heavily for this repair.'

'What repairs?'

And finally there was Mrs Bax up at the top at Number Sixteen: monumentally fat with a boy's cricket cap perched on her thick wedge of stiff grey hair and her veiny flesh spreading horizontally off the striped canvas deck-chair she had set up on the landing on special notches her son had made to give her the best downward view of all visitors:

'Can you spare me a moment, Mrs Peet?' she would drop her ash down the stairwell. 'Do you happen by any chance to know of an Indian restaurant with take-away food? Or are they African, those friends of yours? Hey, how many of them are there up there when you're out at work?' she leaned over and coughed. The pigeons that had wandered in from the street dragging a piece of toast between them scattered at the noise. Mrs Bax threw more bread down and they came back.

'All blacks look the same to me, but I knew they was different chaps each time because they had different trousers and different suitcases. Thirteen different types of suitcase,' she meditated. 'What kind of an agency is it she runs in there when you're at work?'

'She's got friends like everyone else.'

'I bet she has. That telephone hasn't stopped all week.'

'And Africans do have a strong family kinship network.'

'. . . says it's their "strong family kinship network" or something' Flora heard her calling down as she shut her front door. 'Like a slave-galley in there,' calling to the electrician, 'isn't it? I daresay she thinks they hold poetry readings in there when she's out. Hubby'll have something to say' Mrs Bax tossed bread down from her apron pockets. 'Telephone!'

'Stop brainwashing me!' Flora shouted at the telephone when she shut her front door and it started ringing again. Sede was in the bath, so she got there first:

'Hello my dear little girl' a soft voice called down. 'Hello my little simple buzzing bee.'

'What do you want?'

'The dark girl.'

'She's not here. You'd better write to her.'

'Please what is her name?'

'Get off the line.' Flora was still wiping her mouth when her husband came home as though the man had wrapped his lips round it. 'Wrong number,' she explained. The telephone was hot. She washed her hands and washed them again.

'We seem to get a lot of wrong numbers these days.' Or perhaps it was a cross-culture clash or a different conception of the family.

'Or perhaps our number is – say – almost the same as the number of some – say – say –'

'Some railway station. Have you seen my dictionary?' They started looking for it.

'Perhaps Sede borrowed it.'

'Now now. Don't start stampeding me! There's nothing behind there but dust.' Nevertheless they were both peering behind the tall Victorian wardrobe in Reg's workroom. There was something there. They brushed against each other and apologized as nervously as a bachelor and a spinster sent out together on an ill-defined expedition. 'There's nothing behind there but dust' they both repeated, trying to get there alone. But the book wasn't *The Sensuous Woman* or *The Three Hundred Positions* but a small paperback published in Carshalton: *The Meaning of the Glorious Koran*.

'There's something else behind there though too. A stain on the wall. A bloodstain.'

'I expect Sede had a nose-bleed. And sneezed some blood there.'

'Even a Covent Garden Opera singer couldn't deliver a sneeze right behind a Victorian wardrobe.'

'Try not to be such a racist!'

'It's the neighbours who are the racists.'

'I'd avoid those leaky-mouthed neighbours, Sede, if I were you' Flora warned her when she got in. She went to her bedroom. The little radio by their bed was hot and Mrs Bax's oilskin bag full of bread lay beside it. 'Has she been up here?'

'Yes,' Sede shivered, standing in the doorway.

'Please don't let her in. She's a born trouble-maker.' And when Sede looked blank: 'She's a racist I think.'

'Yes, she is,' Sede's face cleared. 'I dropped my key on the stairs and she picked it up and followed me in swearing and fusing all the lights. And she said bad things about you too, and Reg, and I was very angry. She asked me if you treat me all right and she grew very angry when I said where I slept. "That spare room is not fit to sleep in for a young girl. They should let you have the front room." '

'If you don't like the arrangement, perhaps she'd let you have her big front room.'

'That is what I told her, but she said first I must take this room and rent-matter to the Rent Tribunal.'

'But you don't pay rent.'

'That is what I told her, but she just swore and broke round.'

They could hear Mrs Bax laughing with the milkman from her notched-up deckchair at the landing rails above:

'Detail? What do you want a photograph with detail for, if she's your sister like you just said?' The milkman was laughing. Flora tried to picture her 'breaking round'. 'But I'd avoid her if I were you, Sede.'

'That is what I have told her. She is a racist.' But next day they heard Mrs Bax call to Sede on the stairs:

'Hey Sed! Here a moment girl. Can you split me this Jewish half-crown? No? Can't do it? Soppy, aren't you, eh? We're all soppy, aren't we, with this bloody new money. Come in a moment. I want to ask you something. Do they treat you all right down there? Warm enough are you? . . .' There was a big disused fireplace in the corner of Flora's bedroom and she could sometimes hear Sede in the flat below as well as above – Sede and the ex-teacher and Mrs Bax and her son all talking and laughing in queer blasts of draught that came sporadically down or up. They hadn't bargained for this blurred edge to attitudes when they left Rhodesia. The black myth there was a simpler one. And they had given up their sunny garden city, their friends, their position and their children for their version of the myth. Now a barrier came down between them as though they had been jointly cheated. They would look out of the window at the barbed-wired school and stunted young trees barrelled with empty Coca-Cola cans rammed down their trunks. The speckled greening canal seemed to feed its way round between every block in the district, and the pigeons washed backwards and forwards like waves of a dirty sea. It was a vile place. But they could have overcome the smell of the drains and the sight of the red beetles that walked in leisurely pairs up the walls and the filth of the public stair and the air that left black tails hanging from their nostrils if English people had been clear cut. Or if Sede hadn't had so many 'friends and cousins'.

Sometimes at night when they were all three in bed, Flora felt sure she could hear the links on the chain across the front door being winkled and fed one by one along to their eye. She would look out. The hall was silent, but she felt sure she smelt a tobacco smell just the other side of the door.

'What's up?' Reg would ask when she got back to bed.

'Nothing.' He would pretend to be asleep till he thought she was, then he would himself creep to the front door.

'What's up?'

'Nothing.' He still stood there. 'I – just want to say I love you'. He kissed her and put his arms round her shoulder blades and drew himself into her warmth. But he made love carelessly and she said angrily:

'You should give me some warning next time you rape me.'

'I'm sorry.'

'Don't worry. And anyway – she seems too anxious and too innocent for a tart.'

'That's why we left home' he said slowly after a bit. 'We agreed that it wasn't possible to live in a society where there are only two alternative views – the African women as hustlers or Earth Mommas, and the men as thugs with guns. Or saints. That's why we left. For reality's sake.' The phone rang shrilly on its stand in the wall just behind their bedhead. 'Still, I think I'll write to that Bishop what's-it – the one who put a reference in the post two weeks ago. Maybe he'll help find her a job as well. They turned her down again, she says, at the dress factory on account of the colour of her skin.'

'And in any case, what does an educated girl like that want in a dress factory?'

'Corbey, that was his name.'

'Who?'

'The Bishop.'

'And the girls there were dirty, she said, and went to bed with men.'

'Corbey. That was his name.' Reg was just about to write to him next day when a breathy voice came down the phone:

'Pru here! Bishop Corbey's secretary. Could I speak to Sede Angwli?' They could hear Sede's voice coming up the fireplace from the flat below. 'Oh, she's out? Well, no it wasn't important. Just that we wondered when she was coming to see us again and how she's settling down in her new flat. We were all so pleased to hear about it. Sometimes flat-hunting can be terribly hard for overseas students, can't it?'

'Is she a student?'

'Didn't she say she was? I thought someone said she said our "stay" in her country hadn't been such a bad thing after all. But still, my muddle, and I'm glad she's settling down all right. Goodey! The Bishop can use that in the reference he's writing for some old bod. We were racking our brains for something to say and now we've got it: friendliness; adaptability; initiative. Bye-bye.'

The reference they had written flopped on the doormat next morning. '. . . A sweet young woman who has enchanted us on several occasions . . . Mixes well and has made good friends in the white community. You will find her a satisfactory tenant from what I have heard. Corbey – House of Lords.'

The more feelers the Peets put out, the greater their loneliness became. Mr Ahmed Haq, an accountant in Reg's office, shrugged when he tried to consult him:

'A bad class of woman. I know these dark-skinned girls. It will be hard to get rid of her. You English people could call the police and they would take note of your complaints. Alas, not my complaints.' Their English friends were as unsympathetic:

'You've got a lodger stuck in the drain have you? You sucker, Reg! You easy touch. Does she give you a rake-off?' Another friend left the table where they were having lunch:

'I didn't know you had succumbed like that!'

'Oh well' Reg sighed, 'we're on our own. I suppose we must get used to the permissive society over here.'

'But suppose they have guns in that room of hers.'

'Do you exist just to destroy me?' he shouted. Just then the ship's steward called up from below:

'Are you all right up there? There was such a din while you were out – it scared the pants off my wife.'

'My grannie was ill' Sede said shivering when they asked what had happened, 'and her cousins were all so upset I had to comfort them.' She looked ill and distraught.

They had never seen her eat. She refused all invitations to meals with them.

'Sede,' Flora went into her room, 'isn't it time you found a job, and found somewhere permanent to live?' She was lying on her bed reading *Woman's Realm* and watching the 'Los Palmer Show'. The electric fire was scorching her legs but she was shivering.

'I have looked and looked. But they are all racists round here,' she looked at Flora, 'aren't they?'

News of the Peets's capitulation to racialism soon reached other Rhodesian expatriates. Then their Aunt from South Africa heard, and one day when Flora got in from school she heard the strong beat of an African drum-band coming from Sede's room and Aunt Abbie was in there laughing and dancing. 'Ama Bonsu!' They had swapped clothes and were jiving together: 'Ima Abasi.'

'Isn't it wonderful?' Abbie cried waving bead bangles and swinging her goosefleshed arms out of Yoruba cloth. Sede looked less happy in Abbie's Knightsbridge twinset and tweeds. 'It's so lovely to see a familiar face again.'

Abbie had once hidden a Bantu child in her broom cupboard and she hadn't tasted South African sherry or grapefruit since she'd been in England. 'It was so lovely,' she danced, 'to knock on your door and see a familiar black face. It was just terribly terribly nice for me when she opened that front door.' There was a hint of reproach though in her eyes as she said it, and a sterner note when she followed Flora to the kitchen, trailing her Yoruba cloth:

'It was simply very very nice for me. Nothing else Flora. Nothing else. Flora, she's a lovely child, isn't she? And we wouldn't want to do anything to hurt her. She tells me – has she really got to go? Has the rent really got to go up so steeply? I don't want to interfere, but the lady upstairs in the cricket-cap did say – overcharging – Rent Tribunals –'

'Tweedle-dum and tweedle-dee – that's them.'

'I see. Well, I don't want to take sides. But is there anything I can do to help smooth things over?' she picked up a knife and started to peel potatoes for Flora. 'Apropos nothing, my dear, I've lived in Africa all my life and I *know* there aren't these differences between black and white and sagging pinko-grey like me. We are all human beings, the whole world over. At least I think so. I may be in a minority here – I may be the only one in the whole world who dares to say it – but say it I will – Flora, do you think Sede is comfortable tucked away in that corner room all alone? You don't think there's too much draught in there? Why don't you come and join us, Sede?' She stood in Sede's door measuring Flora's prejudice by the smallness of the room and the quality of the blankets on the bed.

'Sede, are those cushions really comfy? . . . Flora, don't you think that mattress is a wee bit hard for such a nice kid?'

'Come and have a drink, Abbie.'

'Isn't Sede going to join us?'

'She doesn't touch alcohol.' They heard her hoovering her floor.

'Flora, do you think we should let our guests do all the donkey-work out there? "Black and White Together" ' she sang, ' "We will Overcome." Come out of there Sede and teach us how to dance. Fill us with magic and music and happiness. Please Flora, please

Reg! Please dear Peets! Is there anything I can do? – Only for three, Flora?' she looked at the supper-table knives and forks. 'Has so much changed since you left Fascist Africa?' her voice dropped. 'Are they turning you round after all? Four people for supper. Surely. Please Peets, four.'

'Sede never eats with us.'

'Perhaps I could change that? Try, at any rate.' Reg stood there with his coat still on reading and rereading a letter he had just received:

'From our estate office. The neighbours don't seem to like the Bleeding Hearts any more than they do the blacks,' he showed the letter to his wife. 'There's been a round-robin on the staircase. A petition signed by everyone except Number Ten who apparently doesn't mind the blacks. Our lease won't be renewed in January unless –'

'Reg,' Aunt Abbie unwound her Yoruba costume, 'I'll go and see them. I'll have a word with your landlord. May I? You see, I come from the Third World so I've got the right to speak out about it. I'll explain to him that Britain is a much more radical and concerned country than South Africa, so you British ought to be doing something radical about race.' Reg put his finger to his nose as if to retain possession of it and stared fascinated as Abbie went on:

'The young are fighting for their rights, and we must fight with them, side-by-side. We oldsters ought to be latching on, that's what I'll tell him. Solidarity! Sede!' she banged on Sede's door. 'Solidarity, Sede! We will overcome!'

'Oh?' Sede stood sleepily in her doorway. 'Oh, I see.'

The Peets laughed as they pictured Abbie at the estate office down the road standing by the frosted-glass partition arguing with the drowsy girl who sat there all day between the electric fire and the board of front-door keys; smiling and reasoning and as close to communication as pins to literacy or sound to patch.

'Sede, it looks as though we'll be leaving here,' Reg said.

'Oh! You mean this flat will be mine after all?' Sede had been filling the kettle and her face broke open and she sat down hugging it and laughing.

'No. We'll all have to go. The neighbours have got nasty about the noise and "multi-occupation" and – and – it's very unpleasant.'

'You mean, they were on *your* side after all? Not mine? I thought they were on my side,' she clutched her face and burst into tears. 'Now what shall I tell those lads? I've promised them now. And the neighbours said – they were so good to me and I thought they were on my side.'

'Side?' Flora was crying too. 'What's all this about sides?' Then she stopped. It was she who had introduced the terminology of sides that had come back at her like this. 'Racist' and 'Right-minded', she had built it herself. It had been a package-deal from the time Sede had sat there huddled by their fire with her big chiming clock and Flora had explained:

'Reg took a big salary-cut to get away.'

A tide of dirt moved slowly up the curtains feeding straight off the traffic exhaust that rose under their windows at the traffic lights. Flora unhooked the curtains and took them down to be cleaned.

'What's that you got there?' Mrs Bax leaned down from her landing above. 'Curtains? Looks more like a bit of mattress ticking to me. What are you going to do with them? Take them to the cleaners! Why can't you do them yourself? Here. Give them to me and I'll put them in my washing-machine. I'll have them in the spin-dryer in no time. Here, come in. I want to ask you something. I'll tell you about this petition. I didn't want to sign. I don't go poking my nose into other people's business, an elderly invalid like me sitting up here like this all day . . .'

'Sede,' Flora went back to her flat, 'we'll fight them over this petition, so play your cards carefully.' Sede stared and went on packing. 'And if they don't renew the lease, we'll all be out together.'

The wind banged on the front door. Bus tickets and cigarette stubs blew against it with bits of rust flaked off the fernwork iron bannisters that a hundred years ago had been a frontier. Sede went on packing. She could only be the injured sun-child or the disintegrating force.

'To say thank you for everything you have done,' she stood there with a present for them – the paperback edition of the Koran. 'I was brought up Christian,' she explained shyly, 'only now I think your religion has lost its powers. That Bible of yours is no good any more. You have translated it too much and it has lost its powers to work miracles. Listen!' They listened to the wind that hugged their block, sucking plaster from between the bricks and grit from the corners and ledges. Another wind hissed up the stairwell. Another punched at their front door again. 'Three separate winds. If there were only one God there would be only one wind,' Sede said softly, 'and one language and one ruler, and the British Empire still holding India and Africa and the whole world. One God and one government and you wouldn't get pushed around by these poor countries, and the United

Nations wouldn't spit in your face. And they push you around in London too, Flora. I've seen them – poor people from poor countries and poor classes – and you have to go out to work now' she ended sadly, 'instead of having black people to work for you as you did when the Bible had still got its powers. And you live in poor places – not that this flat isn't beautiful' she added quickly. 'Simply beautiful, and I am grateful for all you have done. But . . .' The floor shook as a lorry passed. Grit and juvenile pigeon fluff blew under the warped window frame. They watched a row of people half-hidden by lorry fumes huddling below at the bus stop for the bus that never came, and another huddle standing round in a lighted shop with the word 'Surgery' painted across its glass window. 'Poor Flora. Poor Reg.'

'You don't have to go, Sede. We're going to take the whole matter to a solicitor.' But they had lost and she had gone, leaving with them her statue of the Victorian soldier who had brought war and peace to her country, and her pictures: 'Breaking the Ice' and 'The Girls Find the Swans' Home'.

THE LETTER

The Housing Officer's first visit was to the twin sisters who lived in the red tenements that lay alone like a wrecked ship between the clearance sites. She walked down the market street. The pigeons picking at the poultry guts splashed on the pavement clattered up in front of her as she went. A tramp was lying in the doorway of some condemned buildings with his back to the street and his feet in shoes too big for him and tied on with string. A woman was standing with her wig half-off, scratching underneath and calling out cheerfully to a friend:

'Married twice he was, lover-girl, but the effing dog just run out into the sea and knocked his boat over and he was gone.'

From the Bethesda slaughter-house came the sound of chickens screaming like babies, then baying like dogs as they were dragged to death by their legs. The smell of hot blood and burned claw and feathers came from the street as the council vans heaped their incinerators up with refuse. She could see the dressed chickens hanging up to drain like rows of old tights.

'Yes, we're ready to move' the twins told the officer. They had waited behind their front door all afternoon for her visit. 'The place is a slum now and the "meths" get in and try and set fire to the place. But we've taught them to keep their distance and we gave them bottles of water when they were thirsty because they've had their downfalls too. We've had many a downfall ourselves though mother was of the old school tie herself and we are of the new. But the new and the old need each other, don't they? Father had a baker's round before he "went". It was all houses and shops where that junk is lying now. And the people are all gone. They're all the coloured now. The Arabs came to our mother's funeral. We took turns to look after her. We carried the chamber-pot round after her when she got bad in case she needed it. But then in the park one day when it was sunny, well, what could you do? So she never went out after that. Didn't go out any more so we put her bed here by the window and we slept just there beside her. We've always stayed at home to look after mother,' the twins started to cry, 'and now she's gone and no one wants us. We never go out now and we're getting on. So how can we meet men? We've only got what we are. Ourselves. But answer me this, how can she have died and left us when she led such a blessed and holy life?' They wept again. 'She died there in that corner. But why? And she didn't want to go either. She clutched our hands,' the twins held hands and wept again. 'We're forty years old and men don't want us now.'

Brown walls with grave kisses all over them. Shiny brown strips of lino with fluffy edges half nailed down. No clothes lying about, no books or newspapers. No plates. No smell of food.

Outside the sunshine caught a dustbin with an old car tyre laid on top for a lid. A Pakistani woman was sitting in the yard dyeing her hair and calling up to her windows.

'Shall I take you as far as the park in my car?' the Housing Officer asked the twins. 'It's a lovely day.'

'Yes, but that would be presuming on your time and we never presume. We've always kept ourselves to ourselves and we never go out without warning because we always like to look our best. We're forty and the reason why we don't look it is that we never go out without at least two hours' preparation, so that when we do go, we always look like one of the tops. Here is us at our best during the Jubilee.' They showed her a photograph of their red-brick tenement draped in bunting. Crowds of children were leaning over the spiral helter-skelter stairs draped in flags. Hundreds of people packed each long iron veranda, like a theatre packed out on all its six tiers, or like a Mississippi steamer about to sail off with music and bells.

'That's when we was at our best. At his 25th anniversary as King. But we never married and we don't keep having to wear badges to tell you so, do we?' they lapsed into tears again. 'And when the Germans got the butter wharf in the war and it all went up in flames, we all ran to the water to try and get away from the heat. Even the kids jumped into the water at Wapping Steps it was so hot when that butter burned, and the next day the lane was all covered in almonds that had cracked open in the heat. But we don't have to keep wearing badges to tell people so, do we? Did we ever show you this?' the twins cheered up and pulled a framed letter from beside a picture of Jesus floating out of a scallop shell. 'Let's show it to her,' they lifted it reverently off the wall. 'During the war when the underground was bombed our mother had to walk through the tunnel every day to get to work by six. You see she was a cleaner at the printing works in Southwark. She was a cleaner there for forty-three years, and look what they gave her when she left.' They held out the framed letter:

'This is to state that Mrs Teresa (Terry) Wilton has worked here to our satisfaction for 43 years and we have had no reason to complain – Beatons. Printers. Southwark'. 'We were so sorry to hear of your husband's death' someone had added underneath.

The twins held out the reference, breathing heavily: 'And they called her Terry they did, and they give her this when she got too bad and had to leave. So we had it framed, and we shall keep this letter if everything else has to go when we move. Because we're over forty now and we've only got what we are.'

THE DRESS

'Comfort ye!' the boy soprano sang. The tinny, out-of-tune piano in the corner of the playroom clanged.

'Comfort ye, my people!' he adjusted the callipers on his misshapen legs and wheeled his bath-chair a little nearer to the piano.

'And speak ye comfortably to Jerusalem!' Then the angel of the Lord came in on her crutches, and set them at an angle for poising her upright. Someone gave her a candle and she cried:

'Fear not Mary, for I bring you tidings of great joy,' planting her legs apart for balance while the Virgin Mary seated in the middle of the room cried:

'My soul doth magnify the Lord.'

My 'aunt', my 'godmother', my sponsor had warned me that some of the children at the school weren't very strong, were in fact rather delicate and could not walk very far:

'In England all schoolgirls wear uniform,' she would smile over her big glasses. 'There will be riding and tennis and horticulture and archery, and you will study for your School Certificate along with English schoolgirls and boys, and keep up your violin. And in return,' she let paste drip off her paste brush then wiped it clean, 'the Sisters suggest you should help a bit in the school. With the little ones. Some of them aren't very strong. That will be your war work against Mr Hitler, won't it? They are delicate, some of them, and have to be helped a bit . . . Buttons . . . bootlaces . . . Extra fingers and thumbs always help, don't they?'

She smiled over her glasses. She laughed and I laughed. I laughed and she laughed:

'Look, I'm making a scrap-book for them. The pages have to be very light so that they can turn them over easily. So I'm making it from tissue paper. Tissue' she wrote the word down on the newspaper under the glue pot. Each day she taught me ten new words.

'You are a quicky little bird. I'm sure I couldn't have mastered German as you are mastering English . . . At the age of twelve. Still a wee bit nervous are you? . . . Butterflies in the stomach? But I'm sure you'll be happy with the Sisters at school and if you aren't, we'll think again.'

I don't think she meant to send me away. I think she would have liked having a daughter in her bungalow called Pax at the edge of the village.

'I hope it will work out' I could hear her saying softly at the front door.

She had chosen me from the village hall where we refugees had been taken. Someone had taken me behind a screen to get undressed. I could hear the tea cups clattering in the long hall and was sick in the corner and put a chair over it to hide it and sat on the chair.

'One bun each. And one puff,' I could hear her call as the other refugees queued for their tea.

'Here We Come Gathering Nuts and May', we learned to sing.

'Whom Shall We Have to Pull her Away?'

I went behind the screen again to find my cake. My mother had made it and iced it and put it in a tin for me. I lifted the lid and the icing tore off and left a gaping hole in the middle of the cake. The smell of cake and damp pulled crackers and the hot stinging-nettles against the corrugated tin walls of the hall made me go into a corner and vomit again. Then Miss Paul stood there again smiling kindly and shyly behind her big glasses and saying in German:

'Will you call me Godmother or Auntie?'

She was tall and slim and grey-haired and she had a habit of fingering her side-hair and ear-rings as she spoke. She lived alone in a bungalow at the edge of the village that smelt of apples and floor polish and cooking fat, and there were photographs of African villages on the walls and nurses holding up black babies and bishops smiling at black children. There was a *prie-dieu* at the side of the room, in the corner beside the bookshelf. She never used it while I was there, but sometimes I saw she had moved its position after I'd gone to bed or changed the tapestry book-markers in her prayer books.

'May I ask a blessing, Ruth dear?' she would whisper before meals. The food sent up steam that covered her glasses in fat. I would drop my meat between my legs and wrap it in my handkerchief and carry it to the bathroom to hide behind the claw legs of the bath, and sit there till she called me to help her soap the staring celluloid eye-windows of gasmasks stacked in her hall by the Air-Raid Warden, or pick blackberries and sloes from the hedges, or store apples or put down eggs. And all the time the autumn sun came down flat and brown and watching everything evenly.

'Underneath the Spreading Chestnut Tree', we sat knee to knee in the cupboard she had turned into an air-raid shelter.

'Mr Chamberlain Said To Me' . . . 'Ruth dear, we are only practising,' she reassured me when I snoggled and choked and cried silently over the saucers of water we were using to sponge the gasmask eyes. They stared at us like skulls. There were rubber cages with pumps for babies, and Mickey-Mouse masks for infants. 'We may never have to use them, Ruth. This is only a practice.' But I longed for the war to begin, sitting there waiting for my parents in the whitewashed no-man's-land full of eggs and apples and gasmasks and Miss Paul's blurred glasses moving towards me as she whispered:

'Have you spent a penny today? . . .'

'Do you remember your prayers?'

'Miss Paul,' I rehearsed a speech with my dictionary, 'I would prefer to return home to my parents. I would prefer to rejoin them in spite of the danger to Non-Aryans.'

I went to her.

'Miss Paul, Auntie.' She was standing over the cooker making a pancake with cabbage and flour. 'Miss Paul' I said hoarsely; the pancake puffed and lifted and puffed out again in the pan. Steam rose from its middle. Her glasses steamed over again with cooking. Her eyes disappeared. English children were playing in her garden. She was begging them to stay. They were leaning on their bicycles pressing the brakes down. They were banging tennis rackets together and playing 'Animal, Vegetable or Mineral' for me, very slowly, while I tried to compose my speech again . . . 'gratitude . . . hospitality . . . country in which I am a guest' and the low brown sun crept sluggishly everywhere. 'Miss Paul, please . . .'

'Ticklish?' she asked when I stood there. 'Ticklish?' she came at my armpits with her big hands. I hit her face as I threw my arms up in self-defence, and her glasses fell, and trying to catch them she tore my arm with her fingernails. 'We must all try to be very patient,' her voice trembled as she tried to bathe the scratch, 'as patient as the children I was telling you about who are away at school. Mr Hitler has got to be put in his place first, hasn't he Ruth? Hasn't he?' Then she helped me to pack for school.

The trains were very late and full of soldiers and it took us two days to get to Narth. How would my parents know where to come, I wondered, as our train wound further and further into the hills. The halts were small and dark and blacked out. Miss Paul put her head out into the dark at each stop:

'Hallo. Someone. Is this Narth yet?' A porter with a lamp wrapped in blue paper came along the line and helped us down. The air smelt of cold water and pine trees and wood fires. There was water running loudly very near. The black train moved on. The soldiers inside were singing. My godmother was slipping stamps and envelopes and a Jaffa from Jerusalem into my bag. Then her big glasses rushed at me to say goodbye: 'And you will write often and tell me what you need and whether you are happy? Promise? You'll tell me if you aren't, and we'll think again. Promise?'

But I was happy at Narth, and had nothing to write to her except the formula that was put up by Sister Fidelia on the blackboard in the convent refectory on Sunday afternoons:

'Dear Auntie, I hope you are well. I am well and happy. We are collecting cotton-reels for victory. Yesterday was All Saints' Day and we pushed the chairs in a procession down to the lake and Corrie caught a bird there. This morning, a plane flew over . . .'

'My Dear Ruth' my guardian replied, 'how nice to hear from you so soon and to know you are well and happy. How is the violin going? And have you survived the hockey field? I still remember how terrifying "big school" seemed to me when I was your age. Do you need science overalls or anything else? Let me know . . .'

'Dear Auntie, Yesterday was Advent Sunday and we pushed the chairs out to pick fir and holly and made a big round wreath with 25 candles on it. Each day we are going to take turns to light one till Christmas Day when they will all be lit and we will sing: "Watchman Ho! The Bridegroom Cometh" . . . No thank you. I don't need anything.'

'Dear Auntie, Thank you for the Christmas book and sweets and the money. Several committees have kindly sent me cards. No, I don't need anything thank you. On Christmas Eve we had a yule log and when Sister Fidelia lit it, bags of raisins flew out all over the room! And they hid presents all over the ground floor of the school and we pushed the chairs round looking for them. No thank you I don't need science overalls or a hockey stick . . . Today was Epiphany and we had a cake shaped like a king's crown for the Three Kings, and Barry got the ring inside and was crowned king, and we chased the chairs round the courtyard, only he won.'

I didn't tell her how heavy and old-fashioned some of the bath-chairs were, or how frightening some of the children. Several had had meningitis or fits and several lived inside metal frames or had callipers screwed through their clothes. I didn't tell her that several of the children we washed and dressed and carried in pairs between us weighed eight or nine stone, or that the Jewish 'guest-pupils' whom my godmother told me would 'help in the house a bit' wore green-and-white checked maids' cotton dresses and white collars and caps, and that we got up at six in the mornings to sprinkle the carpets with damp tea-leaves and bissell them; that the Music mentioned in the prospectus consisted of standing round the piano in the evenings singing 'Run Rabbit Run' while Sister Fidelia played; that Horticulture meant carrying baskets of soil up from the river to feed the eroded terraces round the convent school and pat round the vegetables till the wind snatched the soil away again in its jaw.

Cookery and Domestic Science meant laying tables and washing up. And for exercise when it was too cold or wet to push the invalids out, we tied pieces of the Sisters' discarded habits round our shoes and smeared them with beeswax from dried-milk tins and skated up and down the long flagged corridors while Sister Fidelia played the piano in the room at the end.

We read to the bed-ridden children and we wrote their home-letters for them, and we learned French with an old Sister with brown stains under her eyes who let us sit round her fire doing crosswords instead, or brush her dog and take him with us on our walks.

Some of the chairs were small with double wheels the children could turn themselves. Some were big canvas awning sheets slung between rusty metal frames. Some were wicker beds on four wheels, and it was very hard to turn these on the winding roads that zig-zagged across the valley towards Narth. Because of this there were certain paths we were forbidden to take.

'That one leads down to the sea,' Renate, another 'guest pupil', pointed out a path where a tree trunk had been laid as a bridge over a rapid green stream. I didn't know there was sea.

Sometimes as we were pushing, Sister Fidelia's cheerful shapeless red face would appear round a bend behind an elderly Sister in a chair. Sometimes we would see their black backs crouched over the wind-torn soil as though they had to crouch there to hold it down. Sometimes as we were finishing a meal at our end of the refectory they would rustle gently in at theirs and we would be ushered out in silent awe. Theirs was a secret life. We might hear their grace or hear them rustling softly on their side of the partition that separated us. But these were the only points at which our lives intersected, and for this neglect I was grateful. I thought of the closeness of Pax and Miss Paul's eyes and her shy way of leaning over and asking if I'd visited 'the dub' today or washed my groins, or tried to eat:

'Just a nippet? A snippet? A bitey? Have you been thinking about things spiritual at all, Ruth? He really *did* come we believe. Just as your great prophets said He would . . .'

'Dear Auntie I am very well' I wrote truthfully. I had felt so guilty at not being a good god-daughter. I had felt raped every time she opened her mouth. I flourished now at not having to be a niece to this kind shy woman in whose home I could only vomit. Here at Narth nothing was expected of me and nothing owed beyond the work the Sisters were too old to do. My war-work till my parents could follow. I was sterilized from fear. Even the bitter winter that came in January was a precise and comprehensible evil.

After Christmas it had grown too cold to leave the refectory. When we had washed up after breakfast we spread blankets on the tables and did lessons there till it grew too cold. Then we pushed the tables back and drew a chalk line on the floor and raced the wheel-chairs round a tennis ball while the invalids waved their sticks at it and tried to shoot it over the goal line. Then Renate would bring in hot cocoa and piles of bread with stewed apple and cinnamon poured on top, and we took turns to have the last impregnated slice of the pile. I was always hungry. I was never sick now. And there was never anything but kindness between these sick children.

After 'break', it was Renate's and my duty to go round from fire to fire with buckets of slag that had been soaked in water and tea-leaves and ashes and egg-shell to keep the fires low and reduce any promising flame to a ribbon of sickly brown smoke. We sat round the grates in silence afterwards in our coats watching the pad of tea-leaves slowly drying out, the egg-shell blackening and the flame suddenly breaking through with a bonk. But there was a war on and one of us was sent for the slag-pan again.

All day in front of the wet fire we froze. We searched for warm corners. We made ourselves mittens of old socks. We filled tins full of hot ash and cinder to hold under our coats. But as the evening came we began to get warm. Our blood began to move after tea, and our chilblains to sing. Scorching worms climbed up through our flesh to the air. We pressed our feet and hands against outer walls. We laid them on the cold slab in the larder, or in a draught under a certain door. We banged them rhythmically to crush the burrowing screaming worms back. We tore at them. We cried for cool. But chilblains were like toothache. They leave no twilight behind. The anguish was new each evening. It was simply a hard winter.

Then one morning when we woke there was light shining on the ceiling and we ran out and put our bare feet in the snow and carried it in for the children to touch and put their chilblains in. The valley was fleshed in snow, and I had never seen a blue sky in this country before. The air was so clear that we could hear the tinkling of the blacksmith's forge three miles away down the valley, and the occasional toot of a steam train standing at Narth.

Or we were woken early by the slither and bump of snow falling off the roof and the drip of melting ice down the rocks behind the house.

We opened the windows. Muslin air came in, and the click of water and the sound of water in birds' beaks. The birds were dripping water and song.

Green moved in the gutters of the black house. Green pushed itself between the hard clinker stones of the walls and the slates of the roof. The world that had been a thin hard silent flat strip underneath our feet was suddenly soft and high over our heads, a ceiling of birds and trees, a noisy forest above.

There were no lessons those days. We wheeled the chairs into the courtyard and stayed there all day. We sat outside the old stables in the sun. Renate threw her maid's starched cap up into a horse's hay-basket and said the war would soon be over. Then she pointed at it hooked up there among the rotting hay and rotting harness and laughed.

Her laughter always surprised me. It was so abrupt and such a scream, like a cat's. And it would come suddenly out of nothing while we were preparing vegetables or deciding whose turn it was to say grace or choose a hymn. Her face was plump and placid and motherly, and when the laugh came in the refectory where she was pouring out tea, I could never believe that it was Renate who had broken the rule of silence with the big multi-coloured tea-cosy shaking in her hand.

Her father had been a fish curer in Munich, she told me, and a rich client had arranged for her to come over to London with his own daughters till the parents could follow. The rabbi would call every week, she was told, and she would be prepared for School Certificate and a nursing career.

They settled near Regents Park. They took Renate to concerts and art galleries and she laughed. Then they told her one day they were going to have their fingerprints taken. They had decided to go to America. They gave her a copy of *Picture Post* and put her on the train to Narth.

'Riding and tennis and science and School Certificate,' she gave her laugh as we sat on the stall wall inside the stables with her cap still abandoned above. School bills that had never been sent out lay in printer's bundles round us – lists of fees for elocution, fruit, flowers, drives and matinées. Archery targets stood in the hay-troughs, the straw stuffing inside them burst and plundered by birds. Fencing masks stood by Kennedy's *Latin Primer* and Indian clubs and logarithm tables.

The Sisters had grown old. The community poor. But the war would soon be over. Hess had landed in Scotland, they said.

We had a sing-song that evening. As we stood round the piano singing 'Boney Was a Warrior' I saw that Sister Fidelia's habit was so thin that her tallow yellowing cotton shift and drawers showed underneath, and when she put her foot on the piano pedal I saw that her schoolboy's shoes were cracked across the toecaps and the heels were as worn as the metal pedals of the piano they were pressing on. But we accepted their fraud.

'When Will You Come Again?' we sang round the piano. I held the page of music to turn as soon as the Sister nodded.

'When the Frost is on the Ground.' She nodded and I turned. 'When the Leaf is Withered,' we sang.

'Where is your home-dress, Ruth?' she asked me as she played. 'Why are you still in your uniform? Haven't you got an "own-choice" dress? What a cat-as-trophe!' she smiled and talked and played. 'Why don't you write to your nice guardian and ask her for one, now that the fine weather is coming?'

'Dear Auntie' I wrote, 'It is warmer now and we are going to make a harbour by the lake and Sister Fidelia is going to lend us her African knife for cutting back the grass etc. Do you think you could send me an "own choice dress" preferably a kilt and blouse?' This was the first time I had asked for anything. I waited three weeks for the parcel, then a letter came:

'My Dear Ruth, How nice to hear from you. And how exciting about your harbour. Best of digging! I hope you strike gold! About the dress, Sister has your clothing coupons and we thought that as you are growing so fast and clothes are so hard these days, you wouldn't mind having a second-hand one to help beat Mr Hitler.'

Sister Fidelia stood there with the dress. I had fancied shorts and a boy's shirt. I hoped at least for a skirt and blouse. The dress that hung over her arm had a black pleated skirt and a mauve and brown striped cotton bib top, and black sleeves – a sort of trick three-piece-suit with jaunty red heart-shaped buttons down the front. She was standing by the gas fire and as it hung over her arm it swayed slightly in the rising heat. The pleated hips shook. The darts up the bib gathered each breast at the nipple like a flower on a stem. Womanhood wasn't in the agreement when I came here. I had asked my godmother for a kilt and blouse and got instead an invitation I didn't want – a preparation for a feast that wasn't mine.

'I think it's rather fun' the Sister said doubtfully, standing there in her safe black. 'And there is a war on, isn't there?' She held the dress against me. The swaying hips and the cute knowing bust took me further and further away from my parents. I didn't want to be a woman when they came. 'The Germans are only the other side of the Channel, aren't they?' the Sister still stood there in her black and white moratorium on sex and time. 'And if everyone only did what they liked, Mr Hitler would soon be here. Shall I ask Renate to come and see what she thinks of it?' she put the dress on my arm like a seal of the future. 'Try it on together.' For the first time there I cried. Renate took me to the box-room and tried to cheer me up.

'Some of the clothes in here are much worse. Look at this!' We had taken to sitting in the box-room during the cold. An old infirm lady had the room next door, and the fire she was allowed warmed the wall right through to the box-room. I leaned against the warmth while Renate held an old lady's dress out. 'She came here to teach music and German but she got ill and couldn't lift the children.' The dress was black crepe with sequins down the front. We could hear her talking to herself next door.

'Frau Benner. She fell one day.'

'And who is Hildegard Henze?' I was stroking a straw suitcase, and reading its label. 'She's not still here is she?' Renate gave her laugh:

'No, she left. Her sponsors were orthodox and very strict and there was anger I think because they wanted her not to sing in the chapel choir, and she wasn't strong and they never called the doctor when her attacks were bad. I think perhaps they were afraid of the bills. So one day when her attack was bad her sponsors took her away. You took her place and her dress. It came in the refugee parcel. I got a yellow handbag and a hat. They have dyed the dress. But it is still possible to see the label.'

We held the label in the neck up to the light. It was dyed brown but we could read:

'Fifth Avenue Junior Miss'. Then in marking ink that had gone mauve like squashed worms: 'Hildegard Henze'.

A bell went for the end of Vespers. Sister Fidelia was in the room we shared when we got there.

'God bless,' she kissed us both. 'Hungry?' she pulled some hot bread from her sleeve. She had laid a butter paper on top and the oil was letting itself down into the hot dough. But I wasn't hungry and I put my share under my bed in my shoe.

I dreamed that night that my parents were in my shoes. They had turned them into boats and were sailing round and round singing 'It's all right.' I sat up and kicked my shoes across the lino. A mouse stared and ran out. The six o'clock Angelus rang. I got up. The air was soft and I had never been out without the wheel chairs before. I took the forbidden path down to the sea. The sea would prove that this was an island with boundaries and shores where people could arrive and leave.

I followed the river all morning. Once or twice I passed sheep-sheds and pens or a burned-out house with black window frames. Then I crossed the shoulder of the hill and the sea was rocking and breaking along the shore and throwing gleaming seaweed intestines on to the rocks. I climbed them to the windy side. The beach here was covered with driftwood, duckboards, old ropes and life-jackets. The whole bay was suddenly covered with sea-litter, old bottles, lavatory cleansers, torn lobster pots. Sea discards blew against my legs, soft, grey palpitating forms of life. The wind grew stronger. Something hit me with a bang. A battered wreath of cotton roses stuck against my leg in the wind. I kicked it off. The wind bowled it back at me. On the hillside above me, among the grey rocks, was a patch of bright-green grass like something accidentally spilt there from a jug. The bright strip was dotted with black beehives. I went towards it. The beehives were the headstones of graves. For centuries the people of Narth had carried soil here before each burial.

Some of the graves were covered with boards and driftwood to stop the earth from blowing away. Their wreaths had been tied down with wire, or set in cages – except for this faded cotton one of limp roses which I fixed back where it belonged under a yellow wooden cross inscribed in scorched pokerwork:

'Hildegard Henze. Aet. 14. In My Father's House.'

'They wouldn't call the doctor,' Renate had said. 'Brown stuff kept falling out of her mouth, and she didn't know me, so her sponsors took her away.'

If the Sisters prayed for the repose of her soul afterwards, they must have done so in secrecy, behind the partition that separated their quarters from ours and away from their 'guest-pupils'' eyes – more afraid of us than of God.

The invalids were sitting in their chairs round the fire when I got back, playing 'I Spy'. One of the children whose head was bigger than his body was trying to lift his teddy-bear off his knee.

'Poor Cassius!' Sister Fidelia picked up the bear when it dropped. 'What did Cassius say when he saw the new baby frogs? I hope he behaved himself. Ruth where have you been?' she seemed to know it was me coming in without turning round. 'Where have you been?'

'To the sea.'

'And what did you see?' she picked the teddy-bear up and put it down. Her big red face opened then crumpled, opened then shut. 'What was there?' she walked me across the room to the door.

'There was a lot of driftwood and refuse and unwanted things.'

'Really? And what else?' We reached the corridor.

'There was a big fish washed up with a tail as big as this.'

'And what else? What did you *see*? What *did* you see?' we reached the box-room door. 'Tell me! Please!'

'There was rope and tin cans and a raft and a bird as big as this.'

'As big as this? And were there sea-urchins and crabs and . . . ?' as she asked, wide-eyed, I could see the Sisters in their green thinning habits strung in a chanting line from the school to the sea with one hand at their hoods and veils – holding them against the wind – and with the other, taking Hildegard on and on, past the pens and the sheep-dip and the burned-out house; taking her further and further away.

The label was cut out of her dress. Then the dress disappeared.

The box-room door was locked. The chapel was locked as well. A big padlock had been put across its doors. The house was in mourning, but through the chapel doors I could hear music and drums. I peered through the keyhole. They had turned it into an ice-skating rink for dwarfs. It was very brightly decorated and cheerful inside, and full of dwarfs keeping watch over their flocks by night. And my parents were among them skating across the ice and waving at me and calling:

'Hullo. It's all right. It was only the ice after all.'

I've worn a uniform ever since Narth. I looked after the invalids until I was eighteen, then I joined the prison service. I've been an officer nearly twenty years now, and I always wear my uniform. Several times I've been put forward for promotion. The last time was for a deputy-governorship – in charge of a whole wing. But it would have meant my own clothes. I thought about it and decided:

'No. I am my brother's keeper. I am my parents' keeper. I am all of you's keeper. All over the world. I am the power you dare not use. You are the dwarfs. All of you. And I am the drum and trumpet and the ice and the rink.'

THE PATIENT'S PLACE

Fog had come down when they reached the roundabout. Major Woods peered ahead looking at the street signs for central London while Lieutenant Duff cleaned the valve of her instrument and talked about the Holiness Hall repairs bill. They had to be back at the Citadel by six to open up the hostel for down-and-outs, and they didn't want to be delayed. But when Major Woods saw the bare arms of a hitch-hiker rearing out of the yellow night air she felt compelled to stop the car.

'Thank you. Most awfully grateful.' The hitcher was tall and thin and wore a short-sleeved cotton blouse and grey flannels. His left wrist was bandaged and in his right he carried a green bag made of the same material as his blouse. 'Super. Smashing' he stuttered in an educated voice.

'How far are you going?' He said nothing. 'How far can we take you?'

'. . . don't mind.'

'But where are you making for?'

'Anywhere' the voice rose slightly. The two Salvationists looked at the young man's smooth white face.

'Have you been waiting long?'

'No. No.' The voice was a clear counter-tenor that blurred from time to time as though it were on the edge of a cry. 'Lovely park' he added as they drove through Epping Forest. 'Smashing park.'

'On holiday are you?'

'On holiday, yes. Just moving around.' The voice managed to be dapper for a moment then lapsed back into a machine-gun stutter. 'Lovely trees . . . Most grateful . . . most kind of you.'

They passed the grey walls of an old institution. 'Prison or hospital?' Major Woods asked herself. The young man's bag touched her neck. She felt something hard inside. They drove in silence for a bit then she decided: 'This is where we turn off,' and stopped the car.

'Most grateful,' he clambered humbly out.

'Will it do for you?'

'Super . . . Most super.' They left the thin figure at a bus stop.

'I just didn't feel safe with him' Major Woods confessed. 'And I didn't like the look of that little green bag. You never know with hitch-hikers who carry so little.'

It was nearly six o'clock when they got back to the Citadel, and they set to and made tea and sandwiches for the dossers who came. There was the dwarf who spent his day at the zebra crossing directing the traffic and shouting out when it offended him. There was the old lady who carried bunches of bomb-site weeds. There was the elderly man in an army greatcoat swinging on a yellow crutch with a torn leather top.

'We can't give you money, dear' the Major told him every night. 'But how about a cup of tea and a bite to eat while you warm up a bit?'

Tea cost a penny and bread another. They had taken the money and finished pouring out when they saw the young man from the roundabout standing at the hall door.

'The Lord must have sent you here . . . You look very cold' Major Woods added guiltily. 'Sit down and have some tea and I'll see if I can find you a sweater . . . Have you got a bed for the night?'

'. . . don't mind.'

'It's only simple accommodation. Some of the men are rather rough and some are a bit simple but the Lord Jesus' hand is on them all. Lieutenant Duff is just going round to open the hostel now.'

'Super.'

'It's not that anyone has been naughty or dirty,' the Major watched the Lieutenant swabbing the floor. 'It's just that, like everywhere in this part of London, the place is falling apart. What is your name?'

'Cretley. Netley. Wetley.'

'And your first name?'

'W. William.'

The hostel was a disused school. They went in at a gate marked 'Infants'.

'Take you to the Cleansing Station, I would' a woman shouted after them as they went in. Waiting in the playground was a man with a pram full of dirty bottles. He had weaved newspapers into the railings to make himself a shelter from the wind.

'Here we are, Mr Colt' the Lieutenant called to him as she unlocked the school doors.

'Very beautiful,' William Cretley stared at the unplastered brick walls and the glittering mica steps and the pigeons squirming along the window-ledges in soft mutated ranks. The Lieutenant unlocked the cupboard where the kettle and frying-pans were kept. A flushing sound came from the rows of children's lavatories, the sound of chains clinking against brick walls and voices shouting at the men necking there:

'I'll take you apart, I will.'

'Is that your supper?' the Lieutenant looked at Cretley's green bag.

'Toilet things' he replied. She noticed that he hardly ever completed a sentence and hardly ever used a reference to himself. Like most of the people here he spoke chiefly in monosyllables, avoiding words like 'I' and 'You' or 'Us' with their arrogant assumptions, but with a terrible humility clinging to impersonal words like 'tea' and 'kettle' and 'toilet bag' as though they dared not venture into the world of 'I' or 'mine', producing only a chain of neutral-thing words to put in the space between themselves and others.

'I'll show you your bed and then you can come down and get yourself some tea.' The Lieutenant took him upstairs to the ward. Sixty beds with chipped enamel chamber-pots under them stood in four rows between the two stone fireplaces. 'Search the Scriptures' was engraved over one and 'Obey Thy Pastors' over the other.

'It's a little bit old-fashioned I know' the Lieutenant began.

'Dirt everywhere' Cretley replied, sniffing at a jam-jar on the high window-sill. 'Water . . . smell.'

'It's only simple accommodation. Where do you live?' But at the question he put his hand over his face.

'Come downstairs and I'll show you the kitchen.'

The kitchen smelt of Jeypine and the white mutton-fat they were melting down to fry bread in. Trestle tables had been laid with red-and-white check cloths. A big black kettle stood on the stove steaming gently. The Lieutenant pinned up a notice:

'No clothes given out till Thursday. Residents may stay in during the cold weather.'

Cretley sat down in a corner of the room away from the cooking, with his legs crossed daintily and the green bag swinging from his hand.

'Come and give us a hand with this fat-bread, son' someone called over to him. 'Or lay us the table will you? The boxes is over there.'

Cretley got up and laid one knife, one fork and one plate at the far corner of the table.

'Smashing manners they give them these days, don't they?' the man called to his mate, watching Cretley taking bread from the pile in the middle and eating.

'Not too much milk' he instructed the man pouring out the tea. He tipped his tea away and cleaned out the cup. 'Milk . . . smell of mums and minimums.' The men slammed down the frying pans and sat down. 'Shock on the liver might reduce the mini-mums to maxi-mums.' His voice rose in anger for a moment.

'Live and let live' the Lieutenant called.

'One place. One time. Get but thither, there grows the whole pillow full of holes that are whole. There's still a smell of milk inside this minimum cup of tea.'

'Jobs for the morning,' the Lieutenant made a list. 'There's the kitchen to be scrubbed out and the coal to be cleared from the yard and someone has thrown an old pram up into the railings. Can you see it hanging there?'

'The whole place holey. Higgledy-piggledy. A really makeshift place. Dead things everywhere and rotting water. And girls' garments,' Cretley took off the sweater she had given him. 'Girls' garments . . . wash all clothes . . . Can't go stravaging round the bright lights with the smell of women's scent however sent the minimums must be.' His voice rose then dropped.

'Have you been in hospital?' the Lieutenant lowered her voice and asked.

'An indication of present verity,' he replied.

'Which one? Ronksfield?'

'Must have a good wash down to get rid of the higgledy-piggledy smell of female allure. Alluding to alluring . . .'

'Well a wash never does anyone any harm in this part of London.'

Cretley wandered away and came back:

'Pills . . . the nightly tipple . . . the hospital.' His voice dropped.

'Shall I ring them? Would you like to go back?'

'Most grateful.'

The Lieutenant went back to the Citadel and rang Ronksfield Hospital, but they didn't want him back. He had discharged himself, the nurse on duty explained. If he wanted to be readmitted he must get himself rereferred by his GP. In any case, the nurse gossiped, the hospital was coming down soon and they were trying to ease out their long-stay patients. The patients' place was in the home.

Major Woods nodded when the Lieutenant told her. 'If you can find out where his home is, I can drive him back there tomorrow.'

'He might have left his home for some reason.'

'He comes from a good home, that's clear from his voice.'

The Lieutenant went back to the hostel. The men had finished frying and were sitting round the radio at the long red-and-white clothed tables. Cretley was upstairs in bed with a thick grey blanket over him, still calling for his tablets. 'Tomorrow we'll take you home, then you can go to your doctor.'

'Minimums and maximums, everywhere.'

'It's just as well you have a firm base,' the Lieutenant searched for some scissors to cut at the parched leather of a tramp's shoe.

'It's just me bunions playing me up again.'

'There now they can breathe,' she hacked at the cracked leather and relieved his swollen toes. 'Or maybe we could find a bigger pair for you . . . Good night William, and God bless.'

William Cretley's home was a small 1930s semi with a bow-window in front and faded cotton curtains hanging in the windows. It stood out from the rest of the neat suburban avenue with its bushes and paths and crazy paving, because of the old car lying across the ragged front garden.

'How pleased they will be to see you back,' Major Woods drove up to the front door. She rang the bell.

'So the wanderer has returned home,' a cheerful middle-aged lady came to open the door and introduced herself as William's mother. She had come in to look after the children as her daughter-in-law had to go out to work to keep the family together now that her husband was sick. 'It's a cold old time of year for the wanderbug to have caught you,' Mrs Cretley kissed her son and shook hands with the Major.

Chunks of dirty frost lay on the broken windows of the old car in the garden. They had stuck a notice on: 'For Sale £50', but the notice had curled and faded and no longer faced the street. Mrs Cretley readjusted it then ushered them in.

'We want to show William that we can take it' she murmured to the Major as she took her into the kitchen and filled the kettle for tea. 'We want him to realize that his home is always there to welcome him however much he rejects it. In spite of everything, he will always be loved and welcomed back,' she made the tea. 'The home is the basecamp for all worthwhile take-offs.' Just then there was a shriek from the sitting-room. Andrew had shaved Betty's teddy-bear. Mrs Cretley took the tea in and made peace between the children. William sat there with the bear's fur on his feet smiling at the naked bear. The Major sat down in a seat that had originally belonged in a bus. Mrs Cretley sat on a settee covered with a coarse grey ex-army blanket watching her son: 'I always say we must allow the young plenty of freedom just to be themselves. William must do his thing as hard as he needs to. That is why I came over to give a hand. I think that's what's wrong with all these drugs. "One three times a day" the doctor says. But he forgets about the inner journey. I've always believed in giving my children the maximum amount of freedom, so I never interfered. I gave my husband his freedom too. He didn't really want marriage and children whereas I wanted both. So we compromised, didn't we William? and just had you.' William buried his face in his hands. 'I thought that with my husband's good blood and mine, we could create really imaginative-dimensioned children who would respond to the maximum amount of freedom. But I wonder what went wrong, William? You would have thought my experiment would work. Why didn't it, William? Do tell me, please.' She stared at the cheap metal teapot with a cracked saucer for a lid. 'William, is it that I gave you too much freedom, and that you are afraid of it?' Her son went to the door and stood there on one foot with one arm raised. 'Still I'm glad I gave it to you, even if it did mean that you threw up the expensive training I gave you to become a professional person. And what *are* material possessions after all?' She looked at the torn lino on the floor, 'So long as you are really happy as a GLC gardener.' Her voice rose slightly as she poured out the tea. 'I remember the time you decided to leave home when you were sixteen. "Good" I said, and had a word with some friends and got you a bed-sitter. "If you turn out to be the not-marrying type that's because you are creative, and I'm always here to help pick up the pieces." You're very silent and thoughtful, William. What have I done? Is it something I've said, or something I've forgotten to do? Or is it some flaw in my personality? Soon I shall be getting quite a persecution complex if you go on like this saying nothing all the time.

Are you suppressing your fear? I notice that you always sit as far away from me as possible and I've read enough Freud to know how important and threatening a mother can be.' She got up and took her son a cup of tea. He still stood there swinging on the door. 'So I'll keep my big mouth shut.'

'Perhaps' said the Major, 'we should both Sellotape our mouths shut and let William talk for a bit.'

'I had that idea too,' Mrs Cretley nodded and poured out more tea. 'For instance, I was always trying to get him to meet more people, and when new tenants once came to the flat opposite ours I tried to get him to have some fun with them. It was a big block of flats we lived in then and I pinned a notice on our window "Come over to a party" and they came. I tried to drop the hint that William had rather run out of people at the moment, and I had just grilled some sausages and was bringing them in when they said: "Where's the party?" Then they went. "That was a short party" I said. But William got a big old torch and hit me hard over the knuckles. I got quite a nasty bruising. But I wasn't angry. "Knock me over and I'll come up again" I told him again and again. "Try not to feel that you are the aggressive one for having all these bad Freudian feelings." "The only thing that was wrong with him" I told the doctor at Ronksfield "was that he needed to accept this love–hate thing." That's how he met his wife. She was a nurse at the hospital. Perhaps now that you are back home, William, I can start to pick up the pieces again. William, I am here waiting for you.'

Just then William's daughter started twiddling the knobs of a toy plastic transistor radio: 'This is the BBC with your latest headlines' she chanted, 'William Ronksfield has escaped from prison again and is wanted in connection with the Queen's jewels which have been stolen again with some sausages. Also he's been bombing again and this time Mrs Sparkey's legs have come off and her ten children are dead . . .'

'Please don't interrupt' Mrs Cretley begged her granddaughter. 'We are having a family conference here. Major, what do you think?'

'About what, Mrs Cretley?'

'About how we can get the wanderer back into circulation again.' But the Major didn't have the courage to say that the Citadel was justifiably fortified.

'I must be off.' She left ashamed.

'Fuzzy-wuzzy was a bear,

Fuzzy-wuzzy had no hair' Betty waved her teddy-bear at her father as he sat by the fire. 'Dad, why did he have no hair?'

'He was really better off where he was' Gillian, William's wife, sighed when she got home. 'The kids get on his nerves so and there's nowhere for them to play out in this weather.' She started to get the supper and cut her finger as she was slicing some lambs' breasts. She wrapped a handkerchief round and tried to hide it, knowing that he wouldn't eat his meal if he saw the cut. 'He says he doesn't feel real, but if only he would pretend for a bit, then maybe it would come back.' She went into the sitting-room. William had put a coat on because the gas-fire had gone out. 'You know where I keep the silver for the meter' she reproached her husband gently.

'Bang-bang. Shoot you, Dad,' his daughter picked up a banana and pointed it at her father. 'Bang-bang. I'm the mad gunner of Wood Green so watch out, Dad. I said watch out.' William unbandaged his wrist and looked at the slashes he had made.

'Bang-bang. Shoot you, Dad.'

'Tea's ready, Will. A special tea because you have come home. Will, will you come and carry something in?'

William went into the kitchen and stood beside the plate rack separating china from glass and metal from plastic, lifting everything in the room into piles, one soft, one hard; one permeable, one dense, while his wife called his mother and the children, and they assembled at the table. Andrew had dressed up in his mother's clothes again and smeared toothpaste over his neck for scent.

'Get out of that at once' Gillian called. The child threw the dress in William's lap as he sat at table. William got up and went to the bathroom and washed and washed.

'I've got a surprise for the grown-ups' Gillian called up the stairs to him. She produced three glass egg-cups and a bottle of sherry wrapped in a cardigan that she had won in a flutter at work and hidden in the kitchen. 'Will you pour it out, William please?' But he refused to touch the sherry that had been hidden in his wife's cardigan. Their daughter had got out her toy-transistor again and was chanting:

'Quick! Hooray. You're on double stamps today. New panty-hose, you lucky ladies. And snake-skin tights.'

'Stop that and come and have your tea' her mother called. 'William, come down', she stood at the foot of the stairs. 'Shout at them, William.' William came back and the meal began. They sat at the table eating. Potatoes and gravy splashed off Betty's fork and up in her face. Birds sat splashed at the windows, four of them and William staring. The family all stared.

'We must try and share his interests' Mrs Cretley had said. His daughter had written a loving letter to him. His son had made him a cake. Both things stood on the mantelpiece welcoming William home. But he covered his eyes from these loving people who were suddenly trying so hard.

'Knock us as hard as you like, Will, and we'll come up again because we love you.' But he only thought of poppies blooming at his wrists and the grit on his wife's nostrils turning to black soil in which he was planting more humming opium seeds in a hot wind.

He laughed. They laughed too. They all laugh, his son picking up a hot potato and throwing it at the wall. His wife waving a plate. He picks up a chair. 'Throw William, throw.' His family stands there urging him on. But he puts the chair down. His eyes are sticky and blurred and his mouth is dry and he has to sit down and hold the sides of the chair and remember that this is his family standing there with food and plates in their hands shouting 'Throw', and that he is William Cretley, aged thirty-six, ex-GLC employee who in a careless moment had spawned two children one day like brown moles suddenly appearing on the skin, or a rash of damp on the wall that spreads each time that his back is turned. He can see his daughter's flesh leaking through the hole in her tights. Everything about him seems to flow through that hole in the tights and comes to grip him as he grips the side of the chair. Everything has broken its boundaries and flows luxuriously round him, and yet he is supposed to act as though he were Adam naming each species of a measured, schematized world. His daughter is driving some splashed gravy along the table top with her knife. His son sticks a fork into his baked potato and William asks as the steam comes out:

'How much comes out per second? per minute? per hour? and how fast?' A hand comes down and claps the meat plates away and they are sitting there putting spoonfuls of pink against their mouths. He can hear everything growing bigger and bigger round him as they take in the food. He wants to stop the exercise but they go on taking in food and spreading it outwards into faces and thighs labelled 'family matter' as they sit there eating the pink peaked Strawberry Ripple Sundae that Mrs Cretley senior has contributed towards the home-coming feast.

'Smile please. All of you' she gets up and waves a camera at the happy reunited family. The camera clicks. They are eating again. William smiles. 'He is with us again' they think.

'He's feeling better.' They all put in their spoons and smile. The pink peaks of the Sundaes are suddenly five pink teats. The cigarette ash in the ashtray is a horse's turd. The legs of the table are meaty and grained and the poppies growing on his wrist bloom out in stiff black genitals.

'But go on trying to act "as if" ' his wife cries as he tears at his wrist. 'Then perhaps the splinter of ice in your heart will melt.'

'We all have ice in our hearts' Mrs Cretley senior adds. But his eyes crust over again and his throat is parched and he keeps opening it wider and wider to try and get round the words his family are saying as they put down their spoons:

'Lovely tea.' He tries to issue them like the rest:

'Lovely tea.' A lorry revs and backs in the road outside. The lorry leaks out petrol from its waist. The teacher has sent his daughter home early with deep scratches on her face and her waist. The teacher is sitting in the lorry, mouthing in four languages.

'The lorry is the type of all evil' he tries to scream, but the scream goes back into his head and his wife is standing there:

'Only a bad dream, Will. Those pills made you fall asleep again.'

For a moment he is intensely grateful to his wife for hearing the scream he could not utter. 'Scream! Try again! Scream hard, Will' she repeats. They are all screaming because he is pushing them off a high ledge on the rooftops. 'You mustn't be afraid of your violent feelings' his wife assures him as he pushes her down. 'We won't let you down.' Down they go.

He gets up from the chair and tries to push them into the road and the unpossessing dark. But Gillian takes his arm. He tries to prise off the hand that is gripping him, but this only makes her happy:

'Hurt me, Will. It shows you are coming back to life.' He raises his hand. For a moment he stands there robed in darkness, towering with anger, sweeping them off the top of a tower-block as he raises his hand and pronounces:

'The Maxi-mum and the Mini-mum are the prototypes of war. That is the present state of verity, war.'

But they are good people and his wife interrupts: 'Hurt me even harder, Will. I can take it.' They are good people and his mother adds:

'We shall still be here holding the fort when you have done your thing and come back.' They are good people so his anger loses its object. He turns and beats his own head instead and stands at the front door staring at the backcloth of deserted semis that have been dropped there like a curtain.

'You'll need a coat if you are going out.' One of the children runs and gets it. They all stand there buttoning him into it, his wife, his mother and the children all buttoning feverishly while he says in his clipped staccato collapse:

'Most grateful. Thank you. Super. Just a little walk.'

Major Woods drives home wondering why William consented to be driven back home so readily. But William knows all along that he will go home to his family. They are good people. The family does not permit much anger. The Major hears his broken strangled voice as she drives along:

'So kind. Most grateful. A most satisfactory drive.'

GIFTS

She had been studying the violin for nearly six years but she still had no clue as to whether she was making any progress or whether she even had an ear. Sometimes Madame Clos would flip through six pages of her book of studies and say:

'I think we will pass over here a bit. I don't think there is any point in trying to reach double-stoppings.' Sometimes though with passionate concern she would make her pupil spend weeks on a small passage of vibrato: 'You see, it is necessary to take very great care with this so that when you give a recital or play with the orchestra . . .'

'Will I ever be able to do that?'

'Oh yes,' vaguely flipping through the next set of studies.

'When will that be, do you think?'

'One day. I shall tell you soon enough.' She smiled and closed the book and handed it back to her pupil. 'Be careful with that extension on the A. Test it always against the G. Goodbye. *Bon courage*. Till next week.'

Sometimes the pupil thought her teacher was too kind to admit that she had no nervous organization as far as music was concerned. Then when she came out of her Edwardian mansion she would go into a coffee bar and eat cakes with butter spread on them. Sometimes, however, she thought her teacher was too unscrupulous to admit that her pupil was wasting her money while she was only expending a very little time and energy flicking the pages to the next study and crying:

'Sharp! flat! And no *rit* please until the second repeat.' Then the pupil would go into a pub and have a schooner of sherry in a corner where other women were sitting. Once when she was in the first state of doubt and was eating pastries, she found something hard in her mouth, and extracted a heavy brown piece of wood with sharp corners tasting of pine. It looked as though someone had knocked a piece off the sound hole of her violin, but when she peered at the violin under the chintz seat, it was intact. So she put the piece of wood in an envelope to show her professor.

'What do you think it is?' she asked as she unpacked her instrument next week.

Madame Clos drew in her breath and pursed her lips. 'It might be anything' she shrugged. 'Where did you find it?'

'In my mouth.' The professor checked her E string against the piano.

'Then you should take it to a dentist. I unfortunately don't specialize in dental repairs.'

'I was wondering perhaps whether another of your pupils had lost a piece of her violin woodwork.'

'My other pupils are men.'

'Then perhaps you would be so kind as to tell them that this wooden missing piece is here. If that's what you think it is.'

'It might be . . . Still a bit sharp, that A string. Now some open bowing to begin with.' The pupil put the envelope with the sliver of wood inside on her professor's mantelpiece. 'And how have you been practising the harmonics?'

'You won't forget the mouthpiece . . . I mean the sidepiece . . . the bit of wood' she pointed to the mantelpiece at the end of the lesson. Beside the envelope stood a crucifix. She suddenly wanted to ask if she might go to mass one day with her professor. But the professor was closing her books and unscrewing her bow and the lesson was over.

During the next week she came across an old bow of her father's. It was much too big for the violin. It was mounted in silver and had the name of a famous luthier stamped on. She took it to her teacher. 'I've got no use for it, if you'd like to have it.'

Madame Clos held it up to the light and examined the position of its spring. Then she put it on the mantelpiece beside the piece of wood her pupil had found in her mouth. Next week she brought a pile of her father's old music. It was an old rare edition that music magazines often advertised for. 'I was thinking it might interest you. These old readings and fingerings.' The professor bowed her head and laid the faded sheets beside the bow on the mantelpiece:

'So how have you been successful with B sharp minor?' That lesson was the last but one of the term, and as Madame Clos was telling her pupil how much she owed her for tuition she also told her that next time would be the last as she was leaving the town. She also rang her pupil two days later to ask her to collect her possessions. There was a great deal of stuff in piles round her music room: a broken plastic handbag, a green worn dress, a stuffed dog's paw and a paperback called *Two Eras of British Defence Policy*, headed the pile. The pupil did not realize how much she had accumulated.

'Nearly six years' the professor smiled and showed her the next pile: some underclothes, a belt whose tooth had broken, some faded green curtains, a blow football set, and *How the Monarch Reigns.*

'And I thought I had just left some sheet music and an old bow and a piece of . . .'

'Have you got transport?' Madame Clos interrupted, holding up a rusty fish-kettle and two attempts at a knitted cap. 'May I call you a taxi?' The pupil suddenly felt very ashamed of all the things she had cast here and wanted to get them out of the room without attracting her teacher's attention to them any further. She decided to fetch her camera and ask permission to photograph a very fine William Morris fireplace that stood in the hallway at the top of the stairs of the large mansion block. Then when she had had it developed she would present it handsomely framed to her teacher as a way of saying thank you for her musical instruction, and also to divert her attention from all the old junk being carried away.

But when the pupil had been given permission to take the photograph she remembered she had no camera, and when she went out to buy one, found the only kind that would do justice to the fireplace was an elaborate affair like a great white unicorned horse. And when she had at last got it through the hallway and up the stairs and erected it to fire squarely at the Morris fireplace, she saw it was even more complicated than she had thought, and Madame Clos had to come out of her flat and help sort out its many plugs and antennae and flexes, and carry its electrodes into her music room to fit into her wiring socket.

At last the pupil held the camera up and fired, but the amount of power it used fused the lights in her professor's flat and the pupil had to be content with taking down the measurements of the fireplace as a record of the Morris art work, its height and depth, the size of its entablature and the bricks it was made of, and presenting the list as her parting gift.

'Thank you . . . So have you got everything?' the teacher slung the last of the bulging satchels round her pupil's neck. The room was empty now except for the 'list' on the mantelpiece: the record of Morris measurements. The room echoed hollowly without all the pupil's things. 'Six years is a long time. Be sure to keep your music up. It will bring you great rewards and joy.'

'And sometime I should like to hear you give a recital' the pupil wanted to reply, but because of all the stuff she was loaded with, the professor guiding her down the back fire-escape stairs didn't hear. Compared with the rich red-brick front of the mansions the back seemed very black and decayed like dirty old cliffs clutched and picked by soft grey birds. She went down carefully, trying to avoid the water that was dripping from the pipes and the birds with soft legs rolling and squatting on the ledges. Her arms were full of off-colour plastic bags, odd stockings, rotting torches with fungus batteries, crushed skirts, slimming kits and asthma inhalers. And as she went down, trying to prevent them falling through the squares in the metal fire-escape she heard her teacher Madame Clos, playing the César Franck violin sonata with her daughter. They played with reckless joy.

RILEY'S WRITING WELL

'Paula! Paulie! This *is* nice,' she poured them out two drinks. 'This is nice, isn't it? The only snag being that we haven't been seeing enough of you lately. Not being nasty and things, but you really haven't been giving us good measure. Peter's been grumbling about "not seeing his Paulie" again. No. Unfortunately he's been called away. He was mad about missing you, but there it was. Another lab. crisis. And also I thought it would be a bit of a bore for you to see him when he's not at his best. No. Yes. And the children have been complaining as well. They haven't seen their Pau-Pau either. Oh, you didn't meet them that time you came over at such short notice and we begged and begged you not to touch that enormous pile of washing up. Well then let's go up and have a peep in at the small mammals' house. Only first let's have another drink and hear your news. It's really too bad that we've seen so little of you. There are so many sad people one decides to drop when one gets married in order to see more of the really worthwhile ones that have stayed outside the rat-race. Like yourself. Peter and I have always said that we have a very special kind of relationship with you. Not many friendships could stand up to coming over at such short notice when the *au pair* girl lets us down with a bump. I was wanting your advice about that too. What terrific clothes you always wear. So unconforming and free. I do envy you your open-ended life. I suppose you have any number of theatres and parties and . . . I suppose your bedsitter is often empty for days on end? It's a terribly exciting atticky studio room, isn't it? I don't expect you're ever lonely? And I don't expect you care much about things like the TV and . . . incidentally, if you ever *did* feel like coming over here for an evening when Peter and I are out, the channel knobs are here, and the fridge is always full and the children can be fun if you are looking for copy for a novel or a play. I do envy you your existential life. I'm sure you must be writing a novel or a play. And you mustn't dream of touching the washing up. While we're out. And once the children are in bed they're no trouble.

Now do let's have your news. Mine always seems so banal. Married life does something deadly to you. That's why I thought it wouldn't be fair to you to make you meet Peter when he's not at his best. And doing overtime in the lab. Perhaps while he's out though, I could ask your advice. I desperately need it. My lifestyle is so complicated and depressing. Oh? Oh? Yes, I know. I know. But you are a free person and an intellectual, and you know that however many hang-ups you have, you'll always emerge at the other end a bigger person, whereas I – well, what I want to ask you is this: When Peter and I first married, we were rather conformist – and this is why we are so anxious not to lose touch with genuinely autonomous people like you – Well, my gynaecologist examined me for the best type of Pill. She? Oh I wouldn't have a woman looking after my insides. A man knows how to look after our women's bodies best – Still, you won't be interested in dreary subjects like that. We women get used to thinking of ourselves as things. How I envy you. Well to cut a long story short, I didn't go on the Pill and we got rather pushed into the baby-factory business, and now I'm wondering whether a liberated woman like yourself could give me some advice. You see, last week when Peter was away, Jay Callow and I – Yes, we'd known each other for years, but only last week did we discover that the only thing we wanted in the world was making babies with each other. Paula. Paulie. I'm not boring you, am I? Jay is so angry at missing you, but he's away filming at Bromwich, and Peter's out with his bird. Though I think she'll stand him up soon. Isn't it like one of Riley's when she's writing well? If you were interested in copy for that novel of yours? Oh? But I'm sure you must have one tucked away somewhere. The most ordinary people – anyone can write a book these days. How interesting you look in that Romanian jacket. Oh. Yes, Marks does terrific things these days. But still, I *must* have your advice. Do you think that Dr Spock realizes that unless one's childer can say:

"Exciting, revolutionary hot-pants Mummy!" and:

"I've got ten super Daddies!" . . . I mean, do you think there's a danger that children growing up with the idea of only one Mummy and Daddy might be rather a stale concept? Are we giving them the best image of adult life? And that's the last thing Peter or Jay or I would want. Paula, is this fire too much for you? I could turn it down. Or I could get you some strong black coffee. I know how tired you nine-to-fivers must be. The pace of your city life. That's why I was thinking that sometimes maybe you might like to come over here and relax – I could go over to your room and make curtains and get Daddy to send a hamper of food. Do you like goose pâté? Paula. Paula. I'll turn the fire down. That's better. You see, for a long time Peter and I haven't been making "a go" of it. I did think of suicide. I discussed it with my gynaecologist.' (The speaker lifted a marshmallow to her mouth. Glucose glistened for a moment round her mouth.) 'But that wasn't for me, I decided. And he agreed. Even though the bottom has fallen out of my world.' (She swallowed. Glucose clung to the fine down round her lips.) 'Paula. Paula. If we moved to those chairs by the window. Fresh air. Firmer back support if you're not feeling very well. And to be honest, I'm a bit hung up myself at the moment too. I don't know whether you've ever thought of writing along these lines. But you could use us if you were interested. It would be as valid as one of Riley's when she's writing well. I could give you all the details of our hang-up. Even my diary. And you could tape-record our dialogues – Peter and Jay and mine. And while you were over here with the tape-recorder – and of course I'd see that the fridge was full – do you like iced Asti? – Jay and I could perhaps borrow your studio. We could do something with that room as a sort of return. Curtains for instance, and Jay thinks that the old fireplace – Sorry, no. You were out. The lady in the shop below let us have a peep, that's all. Such a character. Maybe you want to get her into your novel as well? I do envy you your unconforming way of life.' (But just then they were interrupted by voices in the hall below: 'One of those tiresome days when all the cars in Wigmore Street seem badly parked . . . Frankly I think she's in hysteric overdrive . . . Topless to Peking and they accused her of spying . . .') 'Paula, Paulie, they promised they wouldn't come back before – before ten. Let's face it, dreary, ready-made people like that depress us both. Shall we go up and look at the small mammals? Or shall we slip out of the kitchen and over the garden wall and into the back-doubles? The back-doubles can be such fun. Have you ever seen a Chelsea Mews? Then let's go and see, and perhaps if you had a spare key . . . to your studio . . .

Paula, Paulie, I've bought some Mexican cloth in case you were interested. For this exciting studio of yours. Oh. Not well? Shall I get you another pillow? You look better already! And open the window. That's it. It was air you needed. The colour has come back to your cheeks already. A bit of chat. Another pillow, there. Shall I brew you some strong black coffee? That will wake you up. Rather a hurry, Paula dear. Rather quickly, if you can. Jay's waiting. Can you hold your bottom lip up a bit so that the coffee doesn't spill? Open. Woops. Paulie, rather a hurry. Jay will be here at six. If that's OK by you. Can you lift your left arm so that I can slip this pretty Romanian jacket on? There's a taxi ticking away outside too. Waiting to take you to the tube for Sloane Square. And the children are clamouring to see their Pau-Pau. So if you could just lean forwards and fall into it. Woops. Rather shaky on your pins. Oh I'm sure not. Not a sensible person like you. Your type doesn't get addicted, Paula. What a nice sensible teapot and hot-water bottle that is over there. Just fall. But maybe you don't need your bra. Not in these days of women's lib. Fetishism. Nor your panty-hose. Nor your pants. In our permissive age. Just pull this – this – garment on. Over your nightdress. That would be fun. And a coat. And some shoes on those feet as it's cold out. Shall I give each one a gentle kick from behind? Like this. Left heel. Push. Right heel. Push. Left, right. Gently. Mind the door. Now the stairs. One. Two. Shall I go ahead and be ready to guide you from below? Next foot, Paulie. I'm ready for it. Catch you as you come. Still it's much better than being addicted to heroin or anything like that, isn't it? Now you get into the taxi first, and I'll push your legs in afterwards. Can you drive us to the nearest tube? Good. Good. Rather a hurry though. Paulie, I'll buy your ticket to Sloane Square, but where shall I put it? No bag? No gloves? Behind your ear? That would be fun. Woops. Mind it doesn't slip. Now on to the moving stairs. Left. On you hop. But perhaps the escalator isn't all that safe. Suppose I put you against the wall just here by the ticket machine. Now the key. Your key? Oh? Oh dear. Yes, I suppose it would have to be tucked away at the bottom of your bag. No bag? Locked out? Your pills? Yes I see. What a pity. It would have to have been a very special kind of friendship to even think of room swaps like that. A very special kind of freedom. And as we know, we are *all* afraid of freedom. Yes, yes. Still, being hooked on Nembutal isn't like being hooked on heroin or anything like that, is it? I'm sure that once you got over to our place and had a few sessions with the children and played some of our new records you wouldn't feel the need for Nembutal or kicks. Still never mind, is there anyone who'll give you a kip for the night till they've picked your lock? I'd invite you over to us only it wouldn't be very much fun with all those synthetic people there, and Jay says when he meets you he wants to meet you alone. So many women remind him of Riley when she's not at her best. You know – her characters all just puppets. Woops. Woops. If I stand you against this tenpenny ticket machine, then sooner or later someone will come along that you know. I'm sorry it didn't work out. It could have been just like one of Riley's when she's at her best. But instead she's writing badly.'

PRECINCT

When Professor Marsden stood in his battered hat among the hollyhocks, visitors walking round the college grounds took him for one of the gardeners. His tanned, lined, weathered face would remind them of the story about the quads. Five hundred years of mowing and rolling – was it? – that had made them so smooth and green? Tourists would stop and take his photograph, hoping the very words would come from his mouth. The Professor and Mr Larsen, the head gardener, would laugh when they had clicked and gone:

'Well, Mr Larsen, will you *have* me? *That's* the question. Will you take me on when I retire?'

The gardens were so beautiful in June that he would take time off from the book he was writing to work alongside Mr Larsen; under his instructions. And when the time he had allotted himself was up, he would fill his rusty old hat with strawberries or raspberries, chives or tarragon, and carry them across the road to Mrs Larsen and his wife. Their cottages had stood side by side in the lane for four hundred years unchanged. But times had changed, thank goodness, and Professor Marsden would come in and find Mrs Larsen chatting in the kitchen with his wife, or learning how to make quince jelly, and he would smile to think how the young manhandled their times, and insisted on the class-war. Sometimes, he had to ask himself afterwards, was it Mrs Larsen who had just dropped in, or was it the Warden's wife?

'The class-war is something you can choose, or not,' he would tell his wife. He never dared to repeat the thought to his pupils, and they stood very still at his termly parties, and said little or nothing, waiting.

Professor Marsden, it was said, had once knocked about the world. He had lectured to cane-cutters in Demerara, to pygmies at Fazza, and to an assembled harem at Jualong. He had watched riots in Hong Kong, and *gheraos* in Kerala, and had confessed he was sympathetic to the demonstrators. Why not? Conditions were grim there, and the people were justified. 'But here in Cambridge?' he shook his head. 'Surely not. Not here.'

'Parasites, that's what we are,' he would add with a smile, apeing a pupil, 'we academics.'

The college servants smiled back. 'What's wrong with the word "servant"?' he asked his wife. (We're all servants, aren't we, in one way or another?) They were paid well, and got good food and houses into the bargain. Some scouts' families had been in the 'bigger family' for two centuries. Some of them had worked in the college forty or fifty years. When they retired, there was a presentation and a dinner to which everyone came. There was such a strong feeling of loyalty on both sides, of community, that they wanted to preserve. Professor Marsden was slightly irritated by the young when they ignored this need to belong, and the fellowship between two men – say – gardening that ignored class. For the undergraduates had tried to get the scouts to strike for shorter hours and fewer chores: no bed-making, for example, ignoring the fact that a merely monetary relationship between men is not necessarily a satisfying one. 'Nor is it equality,' the Professor would spin his chair round.

He was offering Mr Larsen some strawberries he had picked.

'Look at them! Woppers!' he exclaimed. 'Take them for the wife. I've got to go now. Sorry. Or I'll miss the train. I've got to be up at the Institute at five.'

But he would much rather be staying here by Mr Larsen, hearing his memories, laughing at his anecdotes about the college a hundred years ago when his great grandfather was coachman to the Dean. He would much rather be working quietly here, he said, taking his orders from Mr Larsen, the gardener. Yes, they were a good, loyal, and interesting lot of men and women, and only occasionally one or two of the young ones left. Like Porter, mysteriously. No one had any idea he wasn't fitting in, or didn't like the work. If they had, they would have tried to sort things out. But they didn't have a chance. He gave a week's notice and left. And the Professor had particularly liked him. There weren't many scouts – let alone West Indians – you could talk to about your work, who were intelligent, as well as friendly, and helpful. He remembered how Porter had rung Mrs Marsden the day before the college Christmas Carol service, and warned her that there was likely to be a big crowd. He had reserved their family six seats right up by the choir, he said. And he had. They were just behind himself, Porter, black and handsome in his white surplice in the choir. Porter singing in his fine tenor, a verse arranged especially as a solo for him: '*Ubi sunt gaudia? Ubi sunt gaudia . . .?*'

He had dropped in often after that to do small things about the house and stop for a cuppa with Mrs Marsden, chatting about life. But the incident the Professor remembered most clearly was the capture of the zobie.

He had been sitting in the attic where he worked; had heard the strange tap-tapping at the roof, and gone down and seen this rare African bird crawling miserably over the tiles. The notorious Resurrection zobie. The zobie that Resurrection College had tried to keep for three years, and this time it was on the Marsdens' roof, stretching out its long proboscal neck, tapping and searching.

Porter had been passing, and together they had found a ladder, and together they had put it to the medieval roof, and together they had climbed, and brought the zobie down, and laid it in Mrs Marsden's gardening trug; and together they had carried it back to Resurrection.

Someone with a camera handy had photographed the scene; 'Professor Marsden, Bowmarket Professor of Medieval Studies, and Mr Rex Porter, scout, from Jamaica, carefully lifting the notorious bird back on to the Resurrection rockeries.' The Professor had treasured that photograph. It meant a lot to him. He suppressed the instinct, though, to put it where his pupils could see.

More than the photograph, though, he treasured the talk they had had on the way home that day.

'Are you coming my way? Good!' As they strolled along, the Professor had inquired about Porter's sons, and Porter had inquired about the Professor's work:

'Well, let's face it, I'm just a scratcher at the surface of enormous problems. I'm the chap who dots the "i"s, and crosses the "t"s.'

Porter smiled: 'Well, I'm sure it's not quite like that. These people who say dons don't do anything useful now . . .'

'And quite right they are!' Professor Marsden laughed with genuine good-humour. 'Quite right. We are just men who . . .' he paused and stared round the college gardens. Mrs Larsen was stooping over the roses and triposaria. Another gardener was mowing. One of the scouts came out in a white jacket carrying a tray. A bedder shook blankets out of the window. Another scout came out with a tray full of dirty cups, glasses, ashtrays and bottles:

'Some gentlemen been having an orgy,' the Professor laughed, confident that his good humour was shared. Porter moved his lips only. 'Yes, there are no two ways about it. A lot of parasites we are. What about your two sons? When are they coming up? Are they that way inclined?'

'I don't think they'll be that way inclined.'

'No academic bent?' Porter said nothing. 'I'm sure there's no reason why they shouldn't then,' the Professor went on reassuringly, not sensing that Porter wasn't asking for reassurance. 'Why shouldn't any normal, healthy young man enjoy his time at an ancient university? . . .' Porter looked thoughtful, and returned the subject to the Professor's work.

'Ah, yes. Well. Must I? Well,' Marsden began. It was a tiny, ivory miniature study of the do-it-yourself state. 'You know, our young friends, the anarchists, revolutionaries, Trots, egalitarians, it's a shame they don't read more, because it's all there in the twelfth- and thirteenth-century cities.' He was researching into the events of a year in a North European town, the year after Heuim had won its charter of liberty and independence from its ecclesiastical Lord. 'But let's face it, Rex, it's all very, *very* small beer beside the work *you* do, keeping *this* particular little free community functioning happily.'

'I wish my work were more worthwhile,' Porter had replied wistfully.

'Oh, good Lord! But it is! I only wish *I* dealt in such positive and certain goods as *you* do! I'd give anything to be going up to London tomorrow to quarrel about the price of eggs and bacon, instead of the Exchequer Rolls in 1239.' There was silence. Marsden would not have mouthed such an insincerity even to his wife and daughter. He changed the subject quickly: 'How are the two sons?'

Porter replied briefly and returned to the Professor's theme: 'Would you say that your analysis of those old-fashioned cities and such-like was a critique of the whole system?'

'Analysis . . . Critique . . .' The words reminded the Professor that he had seen Porter leaving the rooms of one of his own students, the slogan-chanting type, with a pile of mimeographed leaflets.

'Come and see *my* analysis,' he wooed Porter away softly, and they went to his study and looked at the photostats of the town-charter of Heuim. Porter studied them with apparent interest:

'That must be a very interesting critique that you've engaged in.' Then he looked at a photograph of the Professor and his wife and child on horseback, holidaying in Wales: 'I should think you'd need a bit of break, after all that.'

'Would you? Would you? Well, let's face it, in my opinion, the young are right to say we're a lot of parasites, paid to scratch each other's backs, and write reviews of each other's reviews.' He had never before talked with a scout like this, and having started, there was no going back. 'Between you and me I'm constantly being struck by our bad faith, here in our ivory towers. For instance . . .' and he told Porter of a little incident involving a West Indian child; of how he, Professor Marsden, had tried to show the lad he was welcome here, had made asses' ears, and chased him round the supermarket, and slipped on the tiled floors and bruised himself badly: 'And the moral, Rex. The moral is – we academics are never quite in good faith. But we must try. Keep on trying!' He stretched his arms round the panelled room:

'Some day I'll go over the Archives with you. If you'd care for that?'

Porter expressed interest. But next week, he had left. He hadn't hinted at anything wrong. Funny. They had no idea in the Buttery and Bursary.

Mr Larsen took the hatful of fruit that the Professor offered him. 'Look I must rush. You won't give me "my cards" if I go now? How long will it take me, do you think, to get to the station, Mr Larsen?'

'Driving, Sir?'

'No. By bus.'

Mr Larsen thought: 'I'll drive you, Sir.'

No, he would take the bus. For one thing, his wife had the car, and for another, well, he liked to keep in contact with the world around him. Cars were such lonely, isolating things. Cars were like ancient universities. When his pupils came to him and told him they wanted to stay on and do post-graduate work, he used to lean forward and say:

'Good, grand! But why not apply for Glasgow or Preston? They need people like you, and, anyway, Cambridge, let's face it, is a pretty unreal kind of place.' He did his best to belong to the real world though. He travelled by bus when he could. He liked to mix with townspeople as much as possible. He liked to have equal numbers at his parties, and his wife and Mrs Larsen would have coffee together at the kitchen table . . .

The Professor changed quickly, and got his bus. He gave his money absently, staring out, wondering what the real world was doing. It was a pity the Council was clearing away the old streets. He had always thought it a pity to push ordinary people further and further away from the city centre and the colleges . . . He had booked to the station, but his thoughts wandered, and when he got up to get out, the bus went right past the stop.

'I said station,' he exclaimed. 'But you didn't stop. You didn't stop. You didn't stop,' he repeated, surprised and almost shocked.

The conductor, a slim boy of about sixteen, giggled and repeated in the Professor's accent:

'I said station, but you didn't stop.' He rang the bus on past the next request. The other passengers tittered.

'You didn't stop,' the Professor cried, bewildered.

'You didn't stop,' the conductor repeated lisping, this time the passengers laughed outright. Two nurses sniggered: 'You didn't stop.'

'I'll take your number,' the Professor protested. But the conductor had slipped his number-badge off, and tossed it to the back of the bus where the nurses, still giggling, caught it. Professor Marsden rang the emergency bell three times and tapped on the window into the driver's cab:

'He didn't stop. I said "Station, please", but he didn't stop.' The black driver, he could see from the back of his head, was smiling, his cheeks extended out beyond his face, and when at last he looked round, it was Porter, Porter shaking and laughing, Porter sneering and driving faster, Porter mouthing:

'How are the effing crested zobies these days?'

Two miles beyond the station, the nurses wanted to get out, so they stopped the bus. Everyone was laughing as they pushed their way past.

'I'll take your number,' Marsden stared at the torn hole where the conductor's badge had been.

'I'll take your number,' the conductor parroted back, putting his thin white face at his, 'You silly old Pam.' 'Pam and eggs,' Porter added, coming round to the side of the bus, and helping the Professor down its steps, singing in his chapel tenor: 'He came down to Earth from Heaven.' The bus was bumbling away, but the passengers were crowded round the back window looking out and laughing. Marsden went back to the station staring at the ground; went into the buffet and had a double Scotch, and then another. The laughter of the crew and the smiles of the passengers mixed with the dead-pan faces of students at his parties. He felt naked, as though a layer of his skin had been peeled off. He didn't want to leave the station buffet. He didn't want to walk along those streets exposed to all those eyes.

A waitress came over and started to swab down his table, pushing sugar and crumbs into his lap. Her face had been patchily pancaked with brown make-up, and pink showed through, and eyes like wet black gaps, and eyebrows stuck along the forehead dirty with mascara and dandruff that fluttered down towards his drink. But he didn't mind. She sneezed and sent sugar along the table and tobacco-ash into his drink, but he didn't mind. He formed several sentences: 'Can I come with you? Will you come with me?' and held out a fiver tentatively, but she didn't hear or didn't understand. Her eyes were the gaping holes in the conductor's jacket, the bit of stuff poking out where his number had been torn off. Her pancake make-up disguised Porter. And the men round the bar were the college-chapel tenors winking and bellowing through their drinks at him: 'He came down to Earth from Heaven'. The Professor walked home with his head down.

'I missed the train.' The strawberries were still piled on the table where he had put them. He ate and ate, pouring on sugar, and watching bombs of cream burst through the juice. He ate more and more. Poured on more and more sugar and cream. Then he saw the strawberries had come from the college gardens full of holes, and eyes, and mockery. He was sick. Who had allowed it? abetted him? egged him on? and emasculated him, till he could only cry plaintively, again and again; amazed and bewildered at the challenge to his world: 'But you didn't stop. I said "Station", but you didn't stop'?

He stayed in bed for a week. He said he had an upset stomach. He heard Mrs Larsen calling from next door inquiring after him.

'Please ask her not to call,' he begged his wife, 'she only calls because she's a college servant's wife.'

He heard them all asking politely about his roses, his raspberries, and the Resurrection zobie. It was all a game they played with him, as though he were a child. His scholarship was a game; his life was a game they played with polite deference. And now, he had struck against someone who wouldn't play, who wouldn't laugh when he said laugh, but laughed without him . . . When he slept, his finger went to his mouth, and in the mornings his wife told him he had been talking all night in his sleep. She said it several times, waiting, but he didn't ask what he had said. His dreams were all of himself as a young man, before he had found his place in society; before he had found the merchants and guildsmen and freemen of Heuim, or his niche in the Senior Common Room.

He got up. He laughed suddenly at the triviality of the incident. He thought of all the barbed retorts he had given in replies to papers, and at seminars – where he was among his peers. He practised blithe, hard, taut replies to cheeky young sprigs. But most of them seemed appropriate only for his peers. Or he wasn't versed in light-hearted anger, and only obscenities came to his lips, not suitable for a senior professor. When, six months later, he found himself on the thin, white-faced conductor's bus, he hadn't yet got hold of the right retort. He had practised for six months, but it wasn't mastered yet.

It was six months later, but they recognized each other. The young conductor stepped back on his platform, whipped off his number-badge, put his finger in his mouth and cried:

'But you didn't stop! I said "Stop" and you didn't stop!'

The Professor gave a laugh. Not the one he had planned though; not the light-hearted, urbane, cut-and-thrust one. But a high thin one that seemed to skid and skate off his vocal chords. He stepped to the door of the bus and waited till he was out and the bus was moving slowly off, then this strange voice came again:

'Go and f— yourself! Unless of course you haven't got one!'

He looked at his hands as though he expected something to be in them. He watched the back of the bus moving away. The passengers in the back seats were staring out but not laughing. He went home quiet and surprised, and sat all day upstairs in the attic room he used as a study hearing sounds outside the window.

It was only a narrow lane with cobbles, but he kept hearing the sound of a bus-engine in it, a huge bus backing up on to the narrow path till it was jammed close against his low medieval window. The room darkened. He didn't dare look out. He went to the far wall and crouched there near the ground seeing them on the top deck, smoking and staring in, six inches from his window-sill, while Porter rattled through his favourite hymns, hitting his driver's cap against his knees, and the narrow-faced boy conductor egged on by the college's junior Fellows and his own pupils, took off his jacket and rubbed his hands together and stepped over the threshold into the precinct: 'We've all come round to drop you one.'

The Professor stood by the wall. Tea, supper, 'Goodnight darling, and you'll turn the thermostat down before you come to bed, will you?' his wife called up. Then he could bear it no longer and went to the window.

'Please don't just stand there. Please come and take me' he shouted out, searching for something between their love and their hate. But his life had made him unable to find that unexploited bit of land. Between the devotion of loyal college servants and the threats of an angry revolutionary proletariat, he couldn't find anything.

A SPOILT LITTLE BOY

'You put your right leg in' they sang, 'you put your right leg out.'

They stood in their little circle holding hands: Robin, Father, Mother, Robin, Father, wiggling their bottoms, lifting their joined arms up and down.

'You put your left leg in, you put your left leg out.' Their legs went in and out, hands swung up and down.

'You do the okey-kokey,' they twisted and turned on the fitted carpet, lifting the child between them, towards the wall and the big translucent green window of the television frame, and, when they came to 'that's what it's all about', shaking themselves, making Robin shake himself, wiggle, wiggle, wiggle.

'Mother wiggling herself' Father pointed out.

'Father wiggling himself' Mother pointed out. 'And then Robin wiggling himself all over. All over. Right up and down.'

Father would help him, then lift him on to his thigh, take him in his arms, and whisper in his left ear. They both looked at Mother and put their hands over their mouths and laughed.

'You put your left side in' she sang. Robin put his left side in, watched his Mother put her left side in; watched his Father put his. Three in. All three sides. This time Mother picked him up after they had finished, and whispered in his right ear. They both looked at Father and put their hands over their mouths and laughed. Father put his head on one side and whispered 'I want to tell you something'. Robin shook himself, put his finger in his mouth, and didn't move.

'Come here, Robin' Father said in a sharp voice. Robin giggled and didn't move.

'Come here, Robin' Father shouted. The neighbours tapped on the wall. Robin went over. 'Where's your hamster I bought you?' Robin wriggled. Father picked him up and whispered in his ear. They both looked at Mother and put their hands over their mouths and laughed. Mother went over to the sideboard and fumbled in the biscuit-barrel.

'Biccy time, Robin. Biscuit and choccy time.'

Robin sat down and ate his biscuit and choccy from the barrel, and a second and a third when she had laid them on his knee, humming and staring at the ground as he ate.

'And it's bedtime for some little man,' Mother put her head on one side, as he chewed.

'Some little man says he won't go,' Father put his head on one side, 'till he's seen the telly man; till Mr Tellyman comes on, eh Robin?'

Robin opened his eyes wide and gave a Noddy smile. Father had a rod with which he could reach from his chair, and poke Mr Tellyman on. Fishing that night. Mr Tellyman was opening the mouth of a very, very big fish he had pulled from the water, prising open its snout wider and wider with his arm. The fish reared up, then was still. The tellyman was pulling his fishing-hook from its jaw with a sound like walnuts being cracked. They watched him ease the hook then tug it clean out.

'Bang. Bang' said Mother.

Robin bounced up and down. 'Bang. Bang.'

When the Tellyman had finished, he got into a boat and rowed away, so Robin got Father's rod and poked the tellyman switch, till he got him standing in a desert with a gun under his arm.

'Bang. Bang. Have they got him, yet?'

'Not yet, Robin' said Mother.

'Robin' said Father, 'where's your hamster I bought you? Where is it? Go and fetch it; go and bring it to Little Mother and me. Show it to me, Robin.'

Robin smiled prettily and said nothing.

Father looked at Mother. 'Little Mother, where is it? Go and fetch the hamster Father bought you.'

Robin went over to Mother and gave her a little push. Father laughed and picked him up, and whispered in his left ear. They both laughed, and Robin went over to Mother and pinched her leg. Mother laughed and picked Robin up and whispered in his right ear. He ran over to the bed shrieking with laughter, and took the counterpane off and dragged it along, and threw it over Father. It covered him for a moment, then it fell off.

'Bedtime for Robin' said Mother.

'But I have a feeling' said Father, 'that someone I know, some little man, doesn't want to go to bed till he's said good-night to Mr Tellyman.' He stretched out for his rod, and leaned over to the television set, and pushed the tellyman up again. Mr Tellyman was kissing. Robin watched for a moment, then he fired at him with the long rod of Father's that had brought the tellyman up. Bang, bang. Kill the tellyman dead.

Father laughed: 'He is a one, and no mistake,' as Robin switched off and on with the long stick, laughing hysterically as he pushed the kissing tellyman off and on, and off.

Father pointed at Mother who was inside the counterpane getting undressed, for it was Beddy-byes for three tired people. Little Mother was getting undressed, and Father was staring at the mauve disc marks on her white thighs where the suspenders had pressed, at the grey girdle with broken steel and rubber ends poking out, her plastic clips and rubber straps, her 'bits and bobs' over which she put her flowered nightie and reappeared smiling.

'It's choccy and biccy time' she said. But Father and Robin took no notice, watching her undress till they saw her rudies.

'Bang-bang' said Father pointing his stick at her, as he had done in the Army.

'Bang-bang' said Robin.

'Robin' said Mother softly. 'I think it's choccy time. Eh? Choccy and biccy time.'

Robin gave his Noddy smile, and went over with his Mother to the sideboard. Father was getting undressed. They came back eating.

'Bang-bang' said Mother.

'Bang-bang' said Robin, getting the rod to push the tellyman on again, but Mother said:

'Beddy-byes, Robin,' and switched it off; 'Bang-bang.'

Robin began to cry and hit his head. He didn't want to go to bed, so Mother said he could have some more choccy and when he went on crying and banging, pushed it between his teeth. 'More choccy-time.'

But Robin was sick of chocolate. He clung to the television, clung to its legs and screamed till they got Father's rod to switch him on again.

'Somebody wants to see my sing-lady,' said Mother.

'Somebody wants to see my bang-bang man,' said Father.

Robin bang-banged at the television till 'God Save Our Queen'. Then the tellyman went without Robin or anyone banging him off. Robin began to scream, to switch, to beat. But the tellyman didn't come back. Father picked Robin up, and tried to comfort him. He was still screaming, shaking like a leaf, so Father got out his own army bang-bang in its big, dark pouch-bag. Robin stroked it, still shaking, then smiled. Bang-bang, he trembled, then was calm.

'Bang-bang,' said Father, looking at the dark of Mother's armpit which was opened to lift Robin away from him. Robin screamed as he saw the soft rudies coming at him, so Father let him open the hard pouch-bag to soothe him, and touch the hard stub snout of the gun. Let him stroke it, lift it, clutch it. Robin's screams became gentle whimpers, and then stopped. Mother tried to lift him up and take him to bed, but his screams started again. So Father let him hold the bang-bang up and point it:

'Bang-bang,' said Father. 'One more bang-bang. Then he'll be ready for his bed.' Robin was quiet and breathing heavily, one hand against his fly, the other in his mouth. Mother came forward again to pick him up, so just to prevent more screaming Father let him lift the gun and point it at Mother's pretty nightie.

'Bang-bang,' Robin smiled and fired, still sucking his finger.

'Wouldn't you say your son was rather a spoilt little boy?' the Coroner asked at the inquest. Father had gone back to the Army.

HYSTERIA, OR RAISING THE ANTE

It was three days now since Strode had barred the door of his digs, gone to bed, and done with everything. It was three days since he had eaten. This was odd. On the third day, he thought, he ought to be in a coma, and not conscious at all except in a pleasant way. But in fact he was perfectly *compos mentis*, and rather bored with waiting for it to happen. Three days since he had spoken to anyone – that is if you don't count the three silent months in which, except for the office typist who brought him his morning coffee, no one had spoken to him, written or rung.

His boss brought him papers to edit in the morning, and Strode returned them in the evening. His fellow lodger, Porter, just agreed with everything he said: 'Ya! Ya!' with a slight smile. Full stop. And once, when Strode suggested going out to a pub, Porter's smile had become almost a laugh: 'Sure! Sure! But not tonight,' and was off on his scooter. Then there was the invitation from the boss to take a meal at Purley Hills where he lived. Strode had looked forward to joining a set at last. He even thought of women; invented a device for remembering names, and an answer for if they wanted marriage. But he was the only guest at Purley Hills, and they talked about a place they all knew in Breconshire, and the dying-out of country lore.

Apart from that evening – silence. So now *he* was opting out. Silence – until someone pushed something brown under his barricaded door, a brown manilla envelope, an advert for shoes, and he had answered demurely, as though he could not help behaving well behind the barricades:

'Thank you, Mrs Bell.'

He should be in a coma, but instead he cried brightly, 'Thank you, Mrs Bell.' He felt no hunger. This was natural. But he felt no weakness either. That was odd. When he got out of bed and walked over to the window to look out, the only bizarre sensation he had was when he fixed his eye upon the chair cover; the design seemed bolder. It seemed to stand out from the cloth in an exaggerated, defiant way.

It surprised Strode too that on the third morning of his absence from the office, no one had noticed, or rung up, or come round. It was against such intruders that he had built the barricade; it was against them that he was going to put up such a fight.

Across the door he had put his trunk, a great, old-fashioned ribbed trunk, the height of a table. On top of that he had put a couple of chairs and his record-player, and then stacked up all his books. On top of all this, as a humorous touch, he had laid a casserole of stewed meat that he had not eaten. It amused him to think of that splashing across the carpet first, cold and smelly, and clammy like toads. Yes, it amused him to think of that casserole being grounded first, and then the expensive record-player. For three days he had lain and wondered which would fall next: the two mighty volumes of Gibbon on the left, or *Pears Encyclopaedia* on the right.

His mind wandered over this subject, reiterating the fall again and again: the casserole, then the record-player, in slow motion. Then he would reverse the motion and let the casserole come to earth second. But all this time, he would rather have been thinking of Asgard, the home of the Gods, where they who had died bravely in battle went. But he didn't. He couldn't. His thoughts went back each time to revenge.

The clock ticked loudly; sounds came from downstairs. He grew angry because he remained so cool and rational. 'I will have to punish you' he whispered, with clenched teeth. He clenched his fist and struck his skull. The skull was surprisingly resilient and he could not get any take off; his fist just bounced off. 'I am afraid I will have to punish you.' He put on a spiteful voice like a sadistic housemaster: ' . . . treat you like a child, inflict a little pain . . . the only thing you seem to understand.' He drank some whisky to give himself courage, then squeezed the glass between his hands. It broke, but though he ground the pieces between his palms, there was no blood, only a rough, white mark, as though he had been stung with nettles.

He looked at his razor, saw a rainbow hue all along the blade:

'Just let away a little of the bad blood,' he explained. 'Bad blood,' he dabbed and watched a little berry of it spurry up from nowhere on his arm. The cut was nowhere near the vein. He knew he was only pretending. He dabbed a little harder, pushed a little deeper, till thin threads of purple sprang from nowhere. 'I'll make them care!' He took a drink of whisky to give himself courage, pressed the blade a little further and wondered why it still did not hurt. Blood, blood. He wanted to see blood. At last it came popping up, flying the length of his arm, suddenly accelerating its pace, and plopping from his wrist to his palm, from his palm on to the sheet, where it made a stain, mauve inside and brown outside, bull's-eye!

He drank a little more, and waved the blade idly, he had at last activated something. Set the world moving. The world, ha! the world! He would teach them. But he saw he would have to push with the razor a good deal harder, and could not.

Someone pushed something under the door, and he heard himself cry politely, 'Thank you, Mrs Bell.'

Suddenly though, Strode was aware that something was different. At first he could not say what; he could only feel it as an uncomfortable weight located somewhere about the thickest part of the door barricade. Then it dawned on him what it was: something had been stuck on the other side of the door. Someone had pinned a notice, or a label, or a joke there. That was it, he knew. They had pinned a label there.

Apart from the over-pronounced chair-covers, the only noticeable effect that three days of starvation had produced upon Strode was that the bed-sitter seemed like his body; the label on the door was attached to him in a painfully personal kind of way. It exposed him to the world, and that he could not tolerate. That was the whole point of the barricade, so he gave a great jerk of his shoulders, hoping to dislodge whatever it was that stuck there, outside. But it was no good. It was pinned firmly into the other side of the door.

He went over to the window. It was the third day, and no one had so much as knocked at his door, let alone found it locked and barred. Yet they had stuck labels there, and it concerned him deeply to get them removed, to have their attitudes brought out, once and for all, into the open. How was he to get at that label? He thought of climbing out of his window and in at the landing one, but this made him feel slightly faint. He wondered whether a sharp blow on this side of the door would dislodge whatever it was that they had stuck there.

No. He rejected both these methods, and, as he stood at the window watching the people passing, it occurred to him to call out and ask someone to walk upstairs and pull whatever it was off the door, fold it up, and push it under to him.

'I say' he called down to the street. 'Do you mind awfully . . .' But it was three months since anyone had spoken to him. Why should they start now? At last, however, a man came over and agreed to come up to the second floor, first door on the left. Strode could hear him climbing the stairs rather slowly, and then he heard the door jolt, and the books give a slight tremor.

'No, no' Strode shouted through the barrage, 'don't touch the *door*. Just take off whatever is written on it and fold it up and pass it under to me.'

But the man just said reassuringly, 'All right, son, soon be all right.' The door went on trembling and cracking.

The man had obviously misunderstood.

'No, no' Strode called back, 'go down to the street again and await further instructions. I suspend all orders. Hold. Hold.' He bawled. But the man only replied:

'All right. Keep calm. I'll get something to break the lock with.'

'No, no. Cancel orders. I want you just to go away. Just push the piece of paper you may find pinned on the door *underneath* the door, and then nothing more.'

But the man had gone, saying: 'Keep cool and we'll shift it,' and came back with what sounded like a heavy tool, and started banging the lock. In despair Strode went back to the window and called to a woman to go up and tell the man to leave off, and then to a boy to come in, and call them both off. Then to a West Indian to tell the child –

Soon the street was being diverted up the stairs of the house.

'It isn't just the lock' their leader was saying. 'All right. Keep your hair on. We'll fix it. Something got jammed.'

'Keep calm,' vibrated down the line of people. 'It's all right.'

Strode dragged at the table, and then at the bed in a last act of defence. He would fight to the last inch, to the last tooth and nail.

But it was too late. They all put their shoulders to the door, and the leader called: 'Heave! Hard!' Down came the stew, the record-player, Gibbon, and the lot. They all paused for a moment and stared with blank faces, then began to trickle away. At the back of the life-line stood Porter, the other lodger. He looked in on the debris with an amused air.

'Oh, Strode' he said, 'someone rang up. Sounded like your boss. Wanted to know where you were. I said I couldn't tell him. Said you'd ring him back. That player's done for' he remarked almost to himself, 'and what a grand smell of pilchards.'

'Pilchards?' Strode cried angrily. 'What on earth has this got to do with pilchards?'

'Telephone then' sang Porter. 'That must be your boss.' He went back down the corridor and Strode was left alone. His soul had certainly been broken open, but not as he had planned. For there was no one there, nothing except the bare landing and Porter in the room at the end, studying his face in the mirror, and humming 'Let the grass grow under your feet'.

What had they done to him, this great mob of people? That was what he could not forgive. They had not torn him apart. But they had not even touched him. He was still alone, as he had been for the last three months, moving through a medium that did not, for a moment, resist him. He put his head out of the window, and swore at some girls laughing down the street:

'You foul . . . Why don't you get yourselves some clean underclothes?'

But they didn't hear him, and went on laughing at something they were reading aloud. And they were gone. And there was silence. The traffic rode past on wheels of velvet. There was nothing all round him but this silence, and the sound of his own guts. Strode began to smile, and then to laugh, leaning out of the window, threatening his revenge:

'If you won't answer me, I'll make you!' He went to the door, to get down there in the street. His landlady was standing on the other side, just about to knock.

'Telephone, Mr Strode' he heard; then his own normal, smiling, polite, deferential voice replying:

'Thank you, Mrs Bell. Right! Thank you! Just coming!'

A KIND OF FREEDOM

I was thirty-five when I discovered that I'd been bought and sold. I discovered it by accident. I couldn't have done so from the faces of people in the street or from my friends. They were as usual. Mrs Havning was in her chair at her front door as usual as I set off for work.

'Bye-bye and look after yourself' she called as usual. No one looked at me strangely on the bus to work. No one looked at me as though I had been picked on, or as though they guiltily knew someone, or some institution, that was punitive towards me. In fact everything was as it had always been ever since I started work at Pead-Luffs. Next year, I said as I had said for twelve years, undoing my office door, 'I'll move on a bit. I'll make a change and find something more interesting.' No, I had said it for fifteen years in fact, and as I was saying it I picked at the pile of letters on my tray, opening and reading one that seemed to be *about* me rather than *for* me. But it said nothing that I could understand. It merely mentioned an agreement that had been made between one Howard Stagg and a certain hospital. I'd never heard of the hospital before. It was somewhere on the Erith Marshes and I decided to ring it up. But the line was engaged for so long that our receptionist grew impatient and sighed and clicked at the line, so I told her that I'd been called out and would be back after lunch. Mr Howard Stagg's address was beyond King's Cross.

'But what I'd like to know' I said, 'is why *you* made the transaction. I mean I would have thought that since it's *my* heart and liver and kidneys that are involved, I'd be the one to consent or refuse, and that it would be me who would get the money. So why *you* rather than *me*?'

'Me? Well it was me who happened to come across you in the telephone book.'

'But does that authorize you?'

'Well, you've got to begin somewhere, haven't you, when you're breaking new ground. I mean, these authorizations are entirely new concepts.'

'But why did you decide to sell *me*? *My* body?'

'As I said, it was I who came across you.'

'But why did you decide to choose *me*?'

'Well, I wouldn't put it that way. I mean we all choose someone whatever we do. Whether we get married or decide to ask someone the time.'

'But why didn't you choose some old lady, Mrs Havning perhaps, the old lady who lives below me?'

'You're young and healthy and full of lovely life. And all businesses have their different perks from the government. Ours happens to be this.'

'Me. But I don't want to give my body away. Even if it's for a good cause. Even if it's for a hospital.'

'No one is asking you to. Your body is property that belongs to you, but one day – not for a long time we hope – it will be public property. Don't look so worried. We're not going to hurt you. I'm not going to interfere with your life in any way. Maybe we'll never even meet again. I'm not going to touch you or even speak to you again after today. Just go on living your natural span of life as you would have done if . . . Just go on living a happy healthy normal life as modern technology allows you to. Enjoy your husband and your children if you've got them. Have more babies if you like. Spin a coin. Buy a new house. Do yourself good. Give yourself a treat from time to time, just as you would do if you were . . .'

'Were what?'

'Just as you would have done before. You're just as free.'

I tried to define my kind of unfreedom and could not.

'You're on to a very good thing if you've only got to pick someone out of the telephone directory to sell' I pointed out to Howard Stagg.

'It's a service. Everything that businessmen like myself do is a service to the community. We service all of you.'

'But how much did they pay you? And *can* one buy another person, even if they don't plan to do them any harm?'

'We keep an eye on you. We look after you, you could say. And some people like the kind of protection and support that this gives them.'

'So it's nothing I've done?'

'Nothing at all. That's not our concept.'

'Could I buy you?'

'In theory. Though in fact you are already a member of our group. One big happy family you might call it.'

'But how will you know when I die? And where? And how will you see that I get somewhere near the Erith Marshes to die?'

'There's no problem there. Any place. Any time. Any hospital. We have an arrangement with them all.'

'So there is no way out?'

'You don't need a way out, my friend. Nothing has changed. You are entirely free. As free as you were before this accidental slip gave you a nasty moment. Nothing in your life has altered. Everything is as it was. So have fun. Maximize your life. Minimize trouble. Go far. Go for the big kicks if you want them.'

'I may be leaving the country. For a long time I've been thinking of changing my way of life.'

'Change it. Change it. There's nothing like a bit of change.'

'You see, mother died recently. And ever since then I've been wanting a change of some sort.'

'Go ahead. Incidentally, *my* mother is very anxious to meet you. I think you'd get on tops with her. You'd click, I know. I'll write her address down and you can hop on a nice red bus and have a good old palaver, just her and you. I'll give her a tinkle and tell her you're coming.'

So I left Howard Stagg's office with the address of his mother. It struck me though that I ought to take some kind of a present to her. I decided to go back to my bed-sitter first and bake her some cakes. I hadn't done any cooking since mother died. In fact I'd been rather at a loose end, I thought. Perhaps it would do me good to go out and visit an elderly woman of mother's age, so I got out the Baby Belling cooker and found the recipe for rock cakes that mother had been so fond of. But as usual when I do any cooking the food tastes all right but it looks all wrong. They didn't look good, the cakes, They were flat and smooth and damp on top and slippery like toadstools without legs, instead of being stiff and dry and rugged and peaked.

Never mind, I thought, wrapping them in some newspaper and sealing it with Sellotape. 'A man on a galloping horse wouldn't notice.' I took the package and got on the bus for Northscape Road.

Number Fifteen was a large Victorian house with a huge conservatory burgeoning on its side. I could see the texts hung on its walls: 'By your fruits you shall be known' in big pokerwork capitals, and 'He who trusteth not shall be cast into Hell'.

There was no one about so I let myself in. Mrs Stagg sat there on a polished mosaic floor in a wheel-chair. She had a cast in one eye, and with the other she gazed at me and at my package of cakes. For some reason I didn't want to give them to her. I could feel the Sellotape sticking to my hands. Both hands were caught in a mess of blotched Sellotape and when she put out her hand to me and said:

'Yes? Yes? What is it? What can I do for you?' I had to proffer both hands. In fact they were stuck together. 'Yes? Yes?' she repeated inquiringly as if to say, 'What have you come for?'

'I thought you might like a bit of fresh air' I faltered, hiding the rock cakes behind a pot plant.

'You can take me to the shopping centre if you want to' she replied, starting to set herself in motion.

The bath chair seemed very heavy and when I lowered it off the kerb to cross the road, I seemed in danger of tipping her out. It was a long walk to the shopping centre and it was already twilight when we arrived. There were the usual shops, a Boots and a Littlewoods and a Stone's Electrical, but to my surprise a funfair had set up in the little piazza they centred on. There was clay-pigeon shooting, Aunt Sallies, coconut shies and knocking naked girls off chairs with wooden balls.

Almost at once, Mrs Stagg won a large pink sanitary towel for throwing wooden balls at a row of hospital beds and hitting the patients' stomachs so that they sat up and sang: 'Till I Saw in my Mother's Eyes'. Then she won a coconut for knocking a large wooden figure of Jesus Christ staggering along under his cross in front of a blue canvas backcloth of the Mount of Olives and sending him toppling into a pond of water underneath. Then she won another prize, this time for knocking off his crown of thorns. The prize was the crown of thorns and it was full of Smarties which she started eating greedily. The next game she was eager to try was knocking him down from the cross with a hosepipe full of water. This seemed to me to be a waste of water in a time of drought and also not to be very reverent. But my attention was taken away from these games by suddenly discovering we were close to the sea.

'I didn't know you lived so close to the sea' I said.

'What?' she drawled. 'What?' eating Smarties out of her crown of thorns which was prickly so that we had to fold a piece of newspaper under it to prevent the thorns from hurting her legs.

I was very hot with all the pushing I had done and wanted a swim. It was dark by now and there was no one on the beach to notice that I had no swimming costume on so I got undressed and stepped into the water.

But it was warm and thick like soft processed cheese. I tried to plunge in and swim, but it was thick and clammy round me. I saw a white breaker rolling in and thought this would refresh me and liberate me from the 'cheese', but the wave seemed to be made of thick Jersey cream still warm and sweet from the cow. It filled my mouth and nose and stuck in my armpits and my pubic hair, and beyond the 'cheese' I could see a huge moon rotting at its lower edge and shining down on the real sea where I wanted to be.

I struggled again to get out of the dairy I was in. The real sea was inky black under the moon, but I could not reach it. I called to Mrs Stagg to help me but she was eating Smarties and 'Wot a Lot I Got' was all she would say, counting each one as she popped it in. I called her again. Perhaps she knew of a boat that would take me out there, or a hovercraft, but she suddenly announced that she was too busy to see me any more and turned her wheel-chair round. There was a little motor at the back and she chugged and wagged away. I could smell the warm sweet smell of cow on me. I could see the beautiful salty sea beyond. The dairy seemed to be receding. If only I could wait for long enough. If only I could wait. It might take hours for the dairy farm to recede. Others must have tried it before me. On the other hand, sometimes I felt that I only had to stretch my arms out and the real sea would have come up to me. I could hear it roaring gently, hissing and plunging. I could hear the plug-plugging of washed pebbles. Could hear it coming forward to lift me and drop me lullingly, lift me again and this time carry me away from my bedsitter and Mrs Havning and Pead-Luffs. The sea was coming, lifting me and dropping me. Then just lifting me under the huge and wasting moon to where beginning and end were one.

WEIGHTLESS

No. They had all gone. Not one of them had stayed with him. Some of them had explained their departure by saying:

'We didn't have the masses behind us in this squat.' Others had said: 'It was a gesture. OK. But it could never have been anything more,' while old Mrs Meard who had lived in the basement for fifty years had been offered a new flat on the Tapwoods Estate, and Miss Tawney who had always said:

'They'll have to carry me out of here feet first' now peered up the stairwell and called:

'What do you all keep opening your cake-holes so much for? First it's this and then it's that and the other. But there's more than just this street, isn't there? What are you going to do about Webber and Gillie and Spakers Row? And what about Buckingham Palace, eh? Hey, old Mr Greaves was ever so upset when they said he got to come. "Give us half a dollar" he said to me. "What for?" I said to him. "To borrow Ernie's barrow to carry me up to St Pancras Burial Ground." And when a funeral went by he stood there and said: "There goes someone who's better off than me." ' But Miss Tawney had gone now too.

They had all gone and the house was empty like an old box that had been kicked round too much. But what would power have been like? How could they have stayed? Could they have taken resistance beyond an Ealing Comedy act in the empty street? – the good-humoured bobbies come to evict them, laying down their helmets on the kitchen table while they took a friendly cuppa? – the characters in the market street throwing up food from their stalls to the barricaded windows of the besieged squatters? – Mrs Meard as the Pearly Queen singing 'On Mother Kelly's Doorstep'? – and Miss Tawney leading the militants to regain the whole street? – invading the empty houses one by one till they had recovered a little island of humanity from the tide of development?

He was the only squatter left in the street and he vowed to stay. They would have to take him down with the walls. The bulldozers might come tomorrow or they might come next month. Or the row of empty houses might stand there for five years till the land was ripe for redevelopment. He went upstairs to the attic to repin the banner they had hung out between its windows. The attic door slammed behind him in a sudden gust of wind. He tried to open it to go down but he found he couldn't. The door handle turned but it didn't engage in the lock. He picked at the keyhole with the lid of his Biro. The rod that janitored the frame seemed to have snapped. He turned the doorknob again then looked for something longer to poke into its works, then for something as sharp as a knife to undo the enamelled screws that held the knob on. He could only find an old lipstick that one of the girls had left. There was no knife in the room, in fact the attic had been emptied when they went. For an hour he scraped at the lock with the plastic lid. Then he threw himself a dozen times against the door. But it was a stout, panelled door and he didn't seem to have enough weight even to make it creak or crack. He sat on the window-sill and thought. Below were the old overgrown gardens with their red-brick walls. Beyond was a bomb-site where cars parked. A girl crossed it with a dog and he called out to her, but he didn't seem to have any voice. The traffic noise from the main road on the other side of the houses drowned it. Beyond the bomb-site were some tenements curving with the street up to King's Cross. He looked down into the garden. Four storeys to jump. He would try to make a rope of the banner slung between the windows, but it was an old sheet and it tore when he tested it. He could lower himself to the next floor if he had a rope and if its windows were open. He tried to bind his trousers and his shirt together but they slid apart as though it were butter and vinegar or oil and numerals that he was trying to bind together. The light-headed feeling grew as he looked over the gathered chimneys of the tenements. In the gap between the two blocks he could see the whitewashed letters on the slate roof of Danby Street Baths: 'Slipper Baths 4d.' In a traffic lull he could hear the slamming of carriage-doors at the station, the hooter of a ship in the Pool, and the sound of water splashing at the Baths. He suddenly thought with nostalgia, as though it were twenty years ago instead of last week, of how he and Jane had gone there and she had grown angry with him for ducking her and had pulled at her bathing-cap till its strap broke:

'You treat all the others like real people,' she had shaken water off herself angrily, 'but me you treat like a doll, like a sexist object, a thing to be fucked every other night. That's all. That's why I shall leave the squat – to go somewhere where I shall be a real person again instead of a mere girl to be fucked.' She spat water from her mouth as it ran from her hair. She spat out water and saliva.

'I'm sorry' he had said, but he knew that he was not regretting the way he treated her but only the fact that she was leaving him. 'But women like to be fucked, don't they? They are always after it,' he tried to make her smile.

'That's typical of you men to live by generalizations about women. Once women were supposed to be so spiritual and above sex that you could make love carelessly, only thinking of your own pleasure. And now the wheel has come full circle and women are supposed to be so greedy for more that you can still treat them as carelessly as a hundred years ago. We shall never get it right until we leave you.'

'But do I treat you carelessly in bed? I thought you always enjoyed it.'

'You made me feel so guilty when I felt nothing. You made me feel sub-human, like a corpse, so that after a bit I didn't dare say what I should have done. I just learned to pretend. And if you didn't want to make love, you always claimed, it was because my legs were cold as a corpse and you were put off, or because I was wearing something unsexy. So you won every way.'

But he wasn't listening. He was thinking of all the times they had made love together, all the times she had screamed out with pleasure, her voice rising higher and higher as he penetrated her. 'Were you only pretending?' he asked her. 'For a year we've been living together and now you tell me you have been pretending the whole time.'

'You were only pretending too.'

'Why didn't you leave me rather than deceive me? Why didn't you tell me you wanted us to make love more . . . ?'

'It would have been like a mouse telling a cat to go vegetarian. It's just not on the cards. In any case you would have accused me of being cold and frigid, and if there's one thing to strike a girl into a panic it's telling her she's frigid. That was how you first got me to come and live with you. You challenged my sex. I was so afraid of being frigid. It's such a final judgement on a woman. You keep us in cages that way. Could I have my ticket for my clothes please?'

'You're going without me?'

'I'm leaving this squat. The women there all lead shadowy lives. The only one who had a real life of her own, Veronica, you accused of gooseberrying on you, so she went.'

'I shall miss you. Please stay.'

'You won't miss me. You'll only miss a doll beside you. I sometimes think you only get an orgasm by thinking of forcing yourself on a reluctant woman and getting her unwillingly with a baby. That must be the fantasy that keeps you going.'

'I didn't think of myself as a sadist. I liked you for yourself. But now you tell me it's all been mimicry. You pretending to be the little woman-mother and me pretending to be the selfless male . . .'

As he looked out of the window and saw the roof of the Public Baths again, he suddenly felt weightless. He threw himself against the attic door but it gave off barely a sound. He might have been poking it with a bit of paper. He got out an old envelope and wrote on it: 'Help. HELP! I'm in the attic of Number 185 and I can't get out.' He leaned out of the window and threw the note out as far as he could. But it only floated down to the garden and lodged on a battered dustbin lid. He wrote another note. This time he wrapped it round the old lipstick case he had found and threw it as hard as he could. The lipstick went over the wall, but the paper detached itself and lay like a feather on top of a shrub. 'Help!' he cried. 'Help!' he waved his arms. 'Help!' he wrote on the banner and slung it out again between the windows. A woman came across the bomb-site and sat down on an oil drum licking an ice-cream and kicking her shoes off and rubbing her feet. Then she fumbled in her bag and got out a wig and put it on. 'Help!' he called out to her, but she was talking to herself, running her hands down her thighs, smoothing out her dress, just talking to herself.

A window went up in the backs of the tenements and a woman put her head out and started to cry, weeping out on to the solitary bomb-site. 'Help!' he called, but she was letting her hair fall over the window pane and weeping. 'Help!' but words no longer had any value. They had talked so much; they had expended so many words in their commune, words like waves lifting up pebbles from a beach under the sea's drift but unable to lift them and take them anywhere. Merely to drop them back again to where they had been.

He had nothing to read, nothing to do except shout out of the window. He paced round the room. His throat was sore with shouting. The room was empty. The brown and green wallpaper was streaked with blood where they had killed cockroaches. Behind a shutter was a note in a shaky old hand: 'Please someone . . . Someone'. He went back to the window. A bride stood on the top landing of the tenements posing for her photograph against the black railings. Then she was slowly descending the corkscrew stairs to a car decked in white that stood waiting for her. It was a windy morning. Her veil floated behind her in the stairwell and he knew as he watched her that Jane had been right about his pretence. She had given him only the illusion of weight. But now it had gone. Everything was a mimic.

But his thoughts were disturbed by a rattling sound. Two knitting-needles were vibrating in a glass jar on a ledge. Was it the bulldozers that were coming near and making them rattle and jump? How long did it take them to get a row of houses down and reach the end one? Would they get to him today or next month? Would they find him if they did? Would they put the bulldozers straight against the faces of the unopened houses and bring his corpse flying down? Or would they go on waiting for five or ten years until the land was ripe?

But he could no longer feel any anger at 'them'. All he wanted was his life back again. He stabbed at the enamelled screws in the lock with a burst of energy. But the lid of his Biro only scraped on its surface. Another mimic gesture. Then he leaned back on his heels and started laughing at what he had done to himself. He had made his gesture but he was the only one who felt its reverberations. The other squatters had been wise. They had preserved their feeling of weight by never having allowed it to be tested. By avoiding confrontation. They had left in order to preserve the illusion of power and freedom. He banged on the door again. He made only a tiny sound. He went to the window and shouted out 'Help!' but the whistling of the starlings on the roof outside was louder. He knew at last what people were up against.

HOSPITAL WEDDING

'Does that swing *still* creak?' the nightnurse folded her apron up and peered down into the airing-court. 'My grandson now he's twenty and when I used to bring him up here as a kid to the hospital "do's", he used to get so moithered if he got the swing that squeaked. "Nan-Nan" he'd cry . . . And it still squeaks and he's married now. Oh well,' she came back to the grill where she was making toast for the junior houseman's breakfast. 'By the way, Dr Hayward, Reggie Dickens is still on about his discharge.' She made the tea and slid the cardboard box of ward case-notes across the polished lino to where the doctor sat reading and eating. 'He says he wants to go back to Claypits, but I keep telling him Claypits went for the clover-leaf overpass. It must be five years ago now.'

Dr Hayward yawned. He'd been called up twice in the night and again at six to check the insulin syringes, then he'd done a couple of hours' reading for his exams. He spread the jam thickly on his toast to wake himself up. The gasfire hissed and dragged him back again to sleep.

It was early June. The swifts screamed round the windows. The sky was a fragile eggshell white. The chestnut trees along the hospital frontier hung like black thunderbolts. The black office kettle shuddered on its ring and puffed. Day and night it sat there. Day and night the blue jets of the gasfire pushed hot thumbs up into the fuggy air. The doctor yawned again and spilt jam; the nightnurse folded some newspaper into a spill and poked it through the green metal fireguard and lit her cigarette. The kettle stirred again. She smoked and pulled the clips from her cap and stared out into the white morning:

'Got your costume for this evening, Dr Hayward?'

Some of the patients were already out there wandering with chairs towards the trees or trailing fairy-lights over the old red sandstone walls or leaning on one leg beside the booths of the funfair that was being set up: bowls and shove-ha'penny, 'Let us help you Jubilate' the notices were already going up. It was the 200th anniversary of the hospital's foundation, and there was to be a fancy-dress after the stalls and raffle and sideshows.

'What are you going as, Doctor?' the nightnurse winked and rubbed her button-nose and folded up her apron and put it away in her oilskin bag. Hayward turned his eyes away from that bag.

'Is that the patients' butter you've got tucked away down there beside your magazine?' he wanted to ask. But the hospital was older and stronger than he was, so he merely made a note in his mind to speak to the chief social worker again about ward food and stared out at the men slowly and painfully lifting the wires of the amplifiers up on to the chapel porch and dragging chairs down the field to the old torn elms that hung in cobwebs beyond the red walls.

'So who's for the chopper this time?' the nurse interrupted him. Her oilskin bag was closed now and she was grinning and executing herself with one of its long broken handles. He stared and she explained: 'I heard the surgeon might be coming down again soon.' She added it casually returning to the ward-report. The doctor stared and went on leafing through case-notes till he came to the patient she had mentioned, 'Reggie Dickens', the name was written in faded copybook on the admission order of over fifty years ago, a speckled blue-lined foolscap with only the top four lines taken by the Justice-in-Lunacy's orderly vertical hand:

'This man fasts and says he has nowhere to go . . . says the hay-trussers steal his blood.' Then with a shock Hayward came on his own unnourished Biro handwriting – a few lines further on but over half a century later:

'Mouth edentulous, tongue furry, abdomen obese'. And on to this the nurses had pencilled their own notes: 'Hospital coat and trousers. Hosp. cigs, birthday and Santa Claus. No next-of-kin'. The doctor could hear their loose hospital shoes against the wainscot outside the office as they queued for a light for their morning hospital Woodbine.

'I Hope I Hope I Hope It's Me'. Music burped abruptly from the amplifiers fixed on the chapel wall. The clock in the tower struck eight-thirty. The nightnurse collapsed her starched cap:

'Well my girl, it's shanks for you.' Hayward watched her cross the walk to the chapel and go behind the graveyard and pack her bicycle and get into her blue nylon supermarket overall with its red shop initials on the lapels and cycle away to her next job. Then he went over to the female side and pulled the bell for admission. He had two hours to get round his patients before Dr Dulton, his Consultant, came to the ward.

This part of the hospital had been built a century earlier and the windows were so narrow that summer and autumn and winter were indicated by what stood on the table at meals and what stood in the big black grates at the ends of the ward. Plants or flowers. Fire or fir-cones. Jam or lettuce. These recorded the passing of the seasons. The days were measured by sounds.

The sound of keys in locks. The food tins being bumped one by one up the stone steps. The counting of cutlery. Plates being stacked. Keys being slid along the lino strip that ran the length of the splintered ward floor, and the endless sound of newspaper being torn into spills and carried slowly and heavily over to the office for a light.

They must have heard the hard incisive sound of male feet on the lino strip because the hoover and polisher were switched off and soft drugged music came suddenly from the satin-fronted box in the wall above the breakfast tables in the corridor where the patients ate.

'There's your day's bread, ladies. And there's your week's marg,' the ward-maid called banging on the reassembled food cart at the top of the glittering steps. 'And there's your morning's sausage. One leg beef and one leg pork. Caught them myself this morning down by the canal. Sister, is it one sausage or two?' She put a chair at the satin box in the wall and hit it with a fish-slice till the music came loudly:

'I Hope I Hope I Hope It's Me'.

'This time three weeks two days four hours and a bit I shall be away on the Costa Brava getting my sun-tan' she added. 'Sister, will you sign please?'

A fair-haired girl with a baby lit a cigarette and stubbed it out against her thigh. A girl with bulging eyes was praying at a small shrine she had opened on the window-sill. A Spanish nurse was trying to coax a teaspoonful of milk sideways into a grey-haired woman's mouth. 'Now come along please Mrs.' The patient's feet and legs parted under the table but her teeth remained locked together. The phone in the office rang and Dr Hayward heard the Sister say:

'Yes, he is Doctor. He's on the ward at the moment.' She came out smiling and fixing her cuffs: 'Good morning Doctor. Dr Dulton asks if you could spare him a moment in the MO's room at ten. I've made some tea in the office', she pressed her hands together.

When Hayward first came to Gledhull from a big London teaching hospital he had been shocked by the unplastered walls and unlagged pipes and mica-stone spiral staircases and the rows of uncleaned lavatories with stable half-doors and the hundreds of slow silent men and women who flattened themselves against the corridor walls as he passed and filed in wobbly queues at bedtime to the dormitory with their big plastic issue bags of possessions under their arms while the nurses lifted back the lockers so that they could get through to the narrow aisles beside their beds. He was shocked by the humble way they lowered their teeth or their suspenders for electric shock treatment if they had been difficult as though they were worthy of nothing else. He was frightened of this meek republic. A few of the patients were aggressive, but most of them seemed to be only against themselves.

'Cheer up, Alex,' Miss Fletton the chief social worker had invited him into her office for a drink. 'Those old people have been here all their lives and they're institutionalized. That's how it takes you after thirty or forty years. But as they die off, those wards will come down. All the younger patients are being oriented back into the community. Watch Gledhull come down in the next two years.' He had been here nearly two years now and he hadn't noticed it. They just used more drugs, he thought as he watched the patients lifting their breakfast sausage heavily to their lips and trying to chew with dried-up mouths.

'I've made a cup of tea, Doctor' the Sister was saying. They went into the office. 'I hear the surgeon's coming down again soon?' she stood on the weighing scales tinkering with the weights and casually asking: 'Is it for anyone on this ward?'

The sunlight had spread in a white scar-tissue across the fields and as far as the grey staircase of the hills. 'It's going to be a lovely day for our do' she added. In the main staircase of the hospital the Matron was searching among old music stands, gasmasks, tin hats and clocking-off machines for sun-hats for this afternoon. She stacked them on a linseed varnished map of the asylum catchment area when they placed it here two hundred years ago in the rich green pasturelands of the river valley fifteen miles from the town. 'What a lovely day' she repeated.

'Got your gear ready for this evening?' the Consultant asked when Hayward went to the MO's room at ten. He sat under the electric-light bulb, reading and seizing mouthfuls of coffee from his cup with strong mobile lips. 'Hi, Alex!' he grinned over his thick jet glasses. His eyes were full and dark and though he was in his middle forties, flesh hadn't yet threatened their expressiveness. 'You've been on Sixteens today?' Hayward nodded. 'Has Miss Gold made up her mind yet?'

'Yes, she definitely doesn't want surgery' he replied as he had done for the last three weeks, each time Dulton had asked. 'She doesn't think lobotomy is for her.'

'Is it because of Di and Pauline? Does she think she'll end like that?'

Di and Pauline had been Hayward's first encounter with personality change. They had been treated by brain-surgery for anorexia and since their return from the Infirmary they had given up drawing and painting and sewing and sat together in a corner surrounded by pin-ups eating sweets.

Once someone had shown Pauline some of the paintings she had done before her operation – dream landscapes, hands with flowers growing out of them, good gates and bad gates:

'Wow-wowey!' she had giggled slowly drawing her hand across her mouth and leaving a black newsprint stain where her paper had brushed against sugar she had stolen from breakfast, 'I shall have to be careful with my past catching up on me like that. I can't even get into my panties now, Doctor.' Her thighs shook as she laughed. 'Just look at me fatties! Down to earth, that's me. Down to brass tacks I'm getting. Still, some men like them that way, don't they Doctor? Pass the humbugs, Di. Give one to the Doctor.'

Her friend Di was barely sixteen when they operated. She hadn't eaten for six months. For six months she had stood at the thick hospital window staring at the jam-jars on its deep brick sill.

'Darling' her mother would call at her when she came to visit, 'please do pay attention. I've bought you three clean sets, now where are your dirties and I'll wash them through tonight?' Di turned for a moment and looked straight through her mother with her big black eyes and smiled serenely at some fluff that drifted past and caught on a splinter of the board floor. 'Darling, please listen a moment. Mrs Norris says she will very kindly come over tomorrow when I can't come . . . Darling, school fees are mounting . . . Darling, we do want to see you back again among,' she looked away from Pauline, 'your own special kind of friends. Our leave is so short and so precious and we do want to see you well before we go . . . Darling, I'm taking you to the hairdresser soon. You do look such a little waif. Something the Salvation Army has picked up. Oh baddy! I shall soon be getting a persecution complex if you go on ignoring me like this, so do please try and pay attention and pull yourself together. And *try* not to be such a self-contained little island. No one is an island you know. And we must see you back at school before we go back to Rhodesia. We know it was our fault all along, darling. We thought that if we gave you love and freedom and a happy healthy environment . . . We thought that if you gave children love and freedom and happiness . . . But now we know. Anyone can be wrong, can't they? Our experiments with freedom were just wrong, and you must try and forgive us. We should have behaved like other people and brought you up conventionally without good schools and pony-trekking and holidays abroad. We slipped up darling, and you must forgive us. And now we are going to let your nice Dr Dulton put your chemistry right again and get you balanced up along conventional lines.' They signed the form for her and Di was taken to the Infirmary and came back ten days later with her temples shaved and a white cap round her wounds. She stood in the ward doorway clutching the Sister's arm and staring round blindly, not recognizing the nurses or her locker or her bed, standing there disoriented till Pauline hooked a chair over with her leg and patted her lap and called:

'Here Di. Over here. You don't want to sit over there with a lot of depressive women. Have a toffee or a mint! Catch!'

They had plastered their corner with pictures of girls in bikinis and were sitting there arm in arm eating when Di's mother arrived again:

'Darling, I've arranged for Mrs Norris to take you to the hairdresser as soon as your mop begins to grow again. And darling *do* try to eat salad instead of all those mucky sweets. And your accent, darling. Would you like to go pony-trekking just on your own as you always used to do before they brought you in here? Do try and pull yourself together a bit darling, now that they've cured you and balanced you up. Try to choose salad at meals instead of all this carbohydrate. And do remember your accent. Will you write to one or two of your old school friends and tell them you're alive and kicking again?'

Di stared at her feet then looked at Pauline and slowly unwrapped a mint and moved it round her mouth: 'Pauline, when you went for "the op." did you have the end bed by the washbasin?'

'Slipped through their fingers she has' the older women on the ward would say, giving the two girls dusters or peas to shell or nominating them to help in the office or give out medicines. But Di and Pauline remained stubbornly in their corner, eating and waiting like brides, and talking softly to each other alone:

'Di, you know the tall doctor with the stoop . . . Di, when you came round . . . did he say to you . . .'

'Pauline, look what I found at the back of the cupboard,' and they would spread old crusts with butter or sprinkle sugar on cake or unwrap a handkerchief of sweet rice mould someone had hidden for the nurses' tea. Sometimes when they found nothing in the ward kitchen they would suck the curtains for the sweet.

'Early days yet' Dr Dulton would sigh. The two girls might have died of malnutrition, he defended himself. Now they would probably die of heart failure. They both weighed over twelve stone. Yesterday Di had eaten a tube of toothpaste.

'Is that why Miss Gold doesn't want to be "done"?'

'She calls it legalized rape.'

Dulton frowned then grinned. Then his elastic mouth worked at the rim of his cup again. 'You know, when I first came here, how they did leucotomy? They gave the patient ECT till his eyes rolled up, then they pushed the scalpel under the eyelids. He had a couple of black eyes for weeks and it was hit or miss whether they severed the lobe or just smashed the whole egg. Things have changed, what?' he pressed back the pages of the periodical he had been reading, ran his firm white fingers down its spine then examined his cuticles as Hayward read:

'A surgical knife which can cut without bleeding by means of a laser beam . . . as easy for surgeons to use as a ball-point pen. . . The development was made by the Atomic Weapons Research Establishment at Aldermaston . . . The light beam seals as it cuts . . . Tests have already been completed on animals and the instrument seems worthy to be put alongside the surgeon's scalpel . . . and has already been used in Australia for brain-surgery . . .'

Then there was another article by a Sydney neurosurgeon who had used the 'knife' successfully for lobotomy on disturbed psychotics. The resulting personality loss had been found to be much less; the grossness and insensitivity much less than in cases performed in the traditional way. 'Especially' the surgeon had observed, 'where there was good initial personality and intelligence and no thought disorder. In these cases apparently personality-depth had not been impaired at all.'

'Try and make Miss Gold see herself as a space-age explorer. An ipsonaut' Dulton was saying as Hayward read. 'Butter her up a bit. Make her feel important. And if she still refuses, then get hold of her next-of-kin and we'll put her under a section and do it without her consent. Try and get it wrapped up this morning because Hennock and his team can come down on the 15th with the laser beam – if I can get the confirmation into the post today. Hennock's very keen to try out this new technique,' he folded his small firm fingers one by one round his coffee cup. 'More coffee?' he held out his other hand. Its whiteness reminded Hayward of a carnivore lily.

'Miss Gold,' Hayward had crossed the ward to where she sat at least four times in the last few weeks, 'could I have a word with you? Have you thought any more about where we go from here? Do you think we are doing enough for you? Or do you think it's time we tried something more positive?' The whole ward seemed to watch for the rite each day. He tried to vary it. 'Sister, could you let us have a room or somewhere private for ten minutes? Sister, would it be all right if Miss Gold and I took a turn on the terrace?' Once he had taken her as far as the old broken fountain and had picked up bits of wood and paper on the way and when they got there had pulled out his matches and lit a small bonfire and watched the flames leap up and make the twigs hiss. Then he had got two flat stones and laid them by the fire and sat down: 'So you definitely don't want this operation? I'll tell Dr Dulton that.' He had sat by his fire watching it move here and there and feeling healed by it. Then Miss Gold had picked up two sides of a cardboard box like pincers, one in each hand and pinched his fire out:

'I think we ought to be returning to the ward.'

'Right.' As they walked back, he could see the patients laughing at him from the top windows. They were still laughing when they reached the ward. Hayward smiled self-consciously at the Sister: '. . . good blow of fresh air' he murmured and sat down at the ward piano and played 'Für Elise'. 'You didn't know I had hidden lights, did you?' There was silence in the room till a patient with a duster and broom eased him off the piano stool to sweep underneath. She shut the lid down and he saw them still laughing at him. 'What are you reading?' he went back to Miss Gold.

Four years of confinement had turned her face the colour of mushrooms and there was a brownish tide round her mouth and a wide white line of scalp where her dark coil of hair had thinned at the parting. She had tied it back with string and stuck the big buttons back on to her sleeves with Sellotape that had turned sick and left a cloudily mucous patch by each wrist. She wore black patent-leather shoes that had splintered like mirrors and turned to grey membrane, and pads were tied on their backs because people trod on her heels, she complained. They knocked her and jostled her, and men tried to touch her genitals and whisper obscene insults. She had delusions of grandeur, ideas of greatness, but feelings of inferiority – never delusions of inferiority, Hayward thought as he read her case-notes. Those feelings were genuine enough, so instead they wrote down 'delusions of persecution'. She had recently knocked a male porter down twenty stairs with an urn of boiling soup. But she didn't want surgery, and she was right enough. People *did* laugh at her. He had heard them in the nurses' office. And he laughed at her himself:

'What are you reading?' he would ask as he approached her on his ward round. She'd been on the same page for as long as he'd been here. The page was dirty and the book's spine was deformed with lying open there at the same place all the time. 'What are you reading?' She put her arm over the page but he leaned over and read:

' "The poet here finds in the visible world (i.e. of the red bus and the glowing windows of the street) a manifestation of that invisible unity and timeless radiance of the eternal moment".' Hayward had read it out loudly. 'Wow' he had said. 'How's that timeless moment going, Sister?'

'Nearly time for a nice cup of tea, Doctor,' the Sister had smiled back, and he had felt ashamed then when he saw them laughing and had added hypocritically:

'Which poet is it, Miss Gold?' But she had merely set her teeth so that there were two deep lines running from her nostrils round the sides of her mouth to the base of her jaw. She crossed her legs and folded her arms over her chest protectively. On the soles of her shoes he could see Elastoplast name-tapes:

'Jean Gold, Ward 16. Toilet and Day-room parole'. The protective pads swung behind. She was right to feel paranoid. She was right not to want a transfer to the pin-up corner.

'Di, when they "did" you, did you have the Doctor with the . . . here, catch!' Pauline broke chocolate into pieces and stuffed it into rock cakes and threw them round the room. 'Catch Nurse! Catch Doctor!

Catch Miss Gold!' Hayward caught his. Miss Gold had hiccups.

'Have you tried twelve quick sips?' he asked her.

'I've asked the nurses several times for something for it, but they won't give me anything.'

'Try my twelve quick sips. Or the back of the cup.' But she sat there hiccupping. There was a field of brown downy silk on her upper lip and he could see the nurses holding her down while they shaved her and harvested it, spun her upper lip into the finest silk for weaving. He could see the hospital 'carding' her away, yard by yard, into degradation. The sky had suddenly clouded over and liquid oozed through a white blister and fell noisily on some shining rabbit hutches outside the window and an old bicycle and pram, and sank into the earth for coal and oil. He remembered he had dreamed last night – a sallow soiled-looking nurse chased him with a teapot out of a house and said it was a home for the dying. And he had gone bathing and the water was so blue he could see the grass at the bottom. It was flood water and he was swimming over the level-crossing and diving down to see if he'd left the city yet and reached the sea. But each time he dived down it was still level-crossing and trains and a notice saying 'Only Street', and he was standing in his bathing trunks by a shitty privet hedge. The clock struck midday.

'Is it *one* bit of haddock each or *two*?' someone was calling the Sister. 'Switch that fan on.' The fan started to hum. Miss Gold stared at it and pulled the hem of her skirt and clutched at the big handbag full of her four years' possessions that she carried with her wherever she went because of theft.

'Does that fan worry you?' Hayward asked. 'It's not a tape-recorder – just a fan,' he touched it with his Biro to make it whirr faster. 'You don't still think people are tape-recording your thoughts, do you? Tape-recording them?'

'No' she hiccupped. It was simply time for her to be discharged. Hayward decided to find Miss Fletton, the social worker, and get her involved against this social rape.

'Ken,' Miss Fletton would cross her long white arms behind her chestnut hair and lean back in her chair, 'Mrs Hussy doesn't want to be discharged to the old people's home and I'm not taking her there . . . Ken,' she would pour out sherry or coffee for Dr Dulton, 'isn't it time we closed that ward at the end? All those men could be out at work . . . Ken,' she would retie the red ribbons that made up her shoes, 'what if Mrs Deeds *is* dangerous? She's not half as dangerous as you and me when we get out on to that motorway out there . . . Ken, those old ladies aren't getting that late supper the kitchen promised them . . . Well, if she won't be admitted without her sister, why don't we admit the sister as well?' Miss Fletton was always the inconvenient intrusion of the outside world into this closed community, and the junior doctors expected every time she went on holiday that there would be a Palace Revolution. But it was they, not she who went each time. She returned sun-tanned and humming with new ideas: 'Ken, why don't we close this whole show down altogether or turn it into a boiled-sweets factory? Ken, half those drugs you prescribe for them get spat down the loo . . .'

'Fay,' Hayward stood in the doorway of the social workers' room. He had never called Miss Fletton by her Christian name before though she called him Alex. He didn't like the carefully manipulated femininity of this part of the hospital. She was sitting there making an enormous satin bow the size of the table while music blurted on and off in the tree outside her window:

'I'm a Little Bit Tired of Saying It'.

'Fay, Miss Gold doesn't want that lobotomy. She doesn't want to be turned into a fat middle-aged bunny playmate any more than you or I would.' Fay lifted the big satin bow and pretended to mount and ride it. The amplifier outside the window gave a sudden high-pitched scream that sent the birds from the trees and the voice came out again:

'One. Two. Three. Can you hear me?' An old man in a tweed suit that covered his hands and feet stood with his head jerked forward beside a trolley of felt hats and flowered sun-bonnets with wired brims and crowns lifting his hands up and down inside his big dog-tooth sleeves.

'This fancy-dress is obscene, Fay. Some of them are already in compulsory fancy-dress for life. Ever since Di and Pauline had their lobotomies I've had this picture in my mind of people who've learned to despise themselves; to see themselves as physical mechanisms; to see themselves as things. And they've even grown forgiving and made friends with the aggression, and what you do to them you do with their connivance. They'll adapt themselves to anything. Those girls go into the kitchens at night and get the night staff to tell them all the crazy things they used to do and think before they were turned into things. They have a ball there every night. I could write an obscene book without mentioning genitalia. It would simply be about giving people what they "really" want as opposed to what they only think they want. Miss Gold doesn't want to be "cured" but it's my job to persuade her she only thinks she doesn't want to be turned into the submissive female. But they'll come out at the end together, she and Dulton, cooperative and dancing. She'll adapt to her fancy-dress.'

Miss Fletton was trimming her eyelashes, sending their fine shredded tips down from a pair of sharp scissors with a crunching sound. Di and Pauline sat on the swing outside. Di's wounds had healed and she'd been taken into Severnbridge to a hairdresser and a cosmetic advisory clinic and she had come back with the world's welcome recorded on her tight sausage curls, sky-blue eyelids and red cupid's bow.

'Let's have a look at you' the staff called to this woman they had made.

'All dressed up and nowhere to go, eh?' Pauline had laughed. 'Come along Di, let's get away from all these depressives.' Hayward and Miss Fletton could hear them outside now on the swing together making rude remarks about the mute old men who wandered up and down, and see them tossing sticks at a defective boy in jeans and a T-shirt with 'I Love You' written on it, and feeling each other's thighs.

'I was mad with Ken about those two girls' Miss Fletton said slowly. 'But with Jean Gold, she's older and . . .'

'. . . unattractive.'

'No, it's not that. She's been here four years after all. And she's no better. How many stitches did that poor bastard chalk up on the stairs when she thought he said he wanted to lay her? She's very paranoid.'

'So would I be if I were forty and non-male and so plain.'

'And she's a nursing problem. She doesn't cooperate.'

'She doesn't connive, you mean. Why should she?'

'That operation Hennock wants to do – it might be a success.'

'The word "success" has a terrible ring these days. Like "adapt".' Miss Fletton was feeding milk from a bottle on to some doeskin shoes on her table.

'I'll have it out with Ken. I agree. He's a bit keen to "lend" her to the surgeon. I'm having a working lunch with him today,' she squeezed adhesive on her eyelids, tested her lashes and put the adhesive bottle back on the shelf between case-histories and hard boots and soft boots and sherry. Outside chairs and benches were being laid round the bright green hide of the lawn with a judge's dais in the middle, and patients were carrying out flowers to tie in the shape of letters and spell out 'Welcome' along the backs of the chairs for the Bishop and the Mayor, and to make a wreath for the winning costume.

Why had the hospital chosen its bi-centenary to mock its patients, Hayward wondered as an aghast white face passed the window in a Tsarist brocade tunic and cap. What would the old lady wear tonight who thought she was the Matron? And the chemist who received communiqués from General de Gaulle? And the headmaster who had become a woman since his wife died? What kind of reality was expected of them tonight? Hayward himself was forced into one kind of make-believe every morning when he got up and went on to the wards. Today's was a game within a game for all of them. What would Dulton wear, and Miss Gold? Perhaps unauthorized costume would be allowed, but he didn't think so. Survival meant Cleopatra, Hitler, Hell's Angels or Samson and Delilah. The hospital was full of home-made lampshades and rugs patterned with sailing ships or crinolined ladies. The paintings on the walls all came from the Red Cross. They waited for a costume or a language.

A shimmer of haze stood on the heads of the barley in the fields beyond the hospital frontier. The sky seemed to have two layers like his last night's dream. He looked through the midday blue to a heavy twilight, and a distant wind came obstinately like the voices of those who remained persistently alive after destruction, clapping their hands and rolling round and calling for flowers and other symbols of survival.

Miss Fletton put a pin carefully between each of her pruned eyelashes and separated them:

'I'll have it out with Ken Dulton at lunch.'

'Thanks.' Hayward went to do his next ward round.

'The gentleman's here again about his mother's putty-coloured drawers' the duty-nurse was giggling in the office. 'That's three times he's called in about those putty-coloured drawers. And Mrs Hitts is on again about her discharge, doctor.'

'And is it on the cards?' Hayward asked. 'I'll go and see her – if you'll tell me – which – she is', he stared at the rows of faces and coloured aprons and chairs and legs that were set along the corridor walls outside. Their midday meal was over and the big food tins were being banged back down the stone steps one by one to the trolley below, but the smell of haddock and sweet tea lingered with the smell from hot parched rubber bed-rings, cast skin and sebaceousness. He lit a cigarette for a moment to correct the smell of hot wet bedding being scorch-dried and scorched dust from the heaters, and that closed glandular institutional smell that they said had hung over this ward for fifty years – of undischarged burdens.

'I'll call Mrs Hitts,' the nurse was filling her handkerchief with sodium amytal bombs for emergencies and pulling at a hairclip on her teeth while Hayward picked the familiar ancient document out of the case-note box:

'Connie Hitts' he read in the Justice-in-Lunacy's dapper hand: '. . . This woman says her husband is unfaithful to her . . . She broods and says the neighbours steal her washing . . .' And again, over half a century later he came on his own formless Biro scrawl: 'Mouth edentulous . . . Breasts nulliparous . . .' then the pencilled notes: 'Hospital frock and coat. Hosp. birthday and cigs'. Then Mrs Hitts was coming over to the office door, lifting the lockers back one by one to get across the dormitory. She didn't look seventy-five. Her face was smooth and clear and moonlike and she had a shock of thick white hair that grew on her neck and shoulders like a hedge. 'No relatives' the notes had said. 'Nobody'. 'And no mind either', someone had added. But Mrs Hitts had borne her life here with dignity. She worked in the bakery and there was still flour on her cheek and sleeve, and a folded apron lay on her arm with a hot loaf inside.

'Please have a seat, Mrs Hitts.' But she went on standing. 'Have a cup of tea. So you want to be off? Where are you thinking of going?'

'Back to Severnbridge sir, to St James, where we come from,'

'St James went a year ago, Connie' the nurse interrupted, giving her a cup of tea that she put away from her. 'Yes, it went for a shopping precinct they wanted round the Abbey. You wouldn't recognize the place, Connie, if you was to go back. And all your friends and relatives have been decanted – out on to the Bendy Lane Estate I think. And who'd get me that nice cup of tea in the mornings before I clock on if Connie went, eh? And what would they do in the bakery, eh? That dough would catch a chill if Connie wasn't there.'

'Very good, nurse. Very good, doctor.' Mrs Hitts turned, bowed slightly, moved towards the gas-jets and poked her trembling spill through the guard for a light. They watched it falter then advance to the flame. It gave the flame a light touch and came out burning. Mrs Hitts saluted them and returned to the room she had lived in since 1915.

'Poor Connie. Her relatives did a bunk years ago. I don't think we'll even get anyone to bury her. Sometimes you don't get anyone in the chapel but the parson and one of the nurses maybe. That street of hers – it's the ladies' toilets now, and the biggest advertisement for cigarettes I've ever seen. There's pink gravel underneath the hoarding, and blue gravel and what-have-you round the sides, and it's got spotlights and floodlighting and barbed wire and notices saying "Keep Off"! It's a big problem, clearance is, isn't it? Poor Connie.'

Hayward left the ward and came out into the sunshine again. Beyond the fair-booths the grass fields had been cut and laid out in hot grey ashes. Beyond them the barley heaved up and down on one long shivering spine, and the bulbous green of the chestnuts seemed suddenly pumped up there and congealed into clots the birds retreated behind. He went to dress a patient's wound and that too seemed to occupy a central cloying position in the universe. The bootlaces he had stitched so neatly across the wrist four days ago had been cut by the nurse and from the eyelets of the stitches red poppies grew. Fields of red poppies with grey sides when the wind shushed. He saw Miss Fletton standing there talking to the Matron. She waved to him and went on talking. He could see her by the great eighteenth-century canopy entrance-hall in a fencing jacket and mask. He went over, but she had gone and was sitting among the poppies with her group-therapy patients, their heads black spikes among the red and grey. Then a boy in a prep-school blazer and grey flannel shorts and cap was dropping a matchbox in front of him, picking it up and dropping it again and again and appealing to the doctor and the group, standing by the coconut shies; beside the notice that said:

'Effort and Endeavour Must Precede Reward' dropping the matchbox like a yo-yo and saying desperately:

'The trouble is I don't know whether I really drop this box each time, or whether I only think I do. Maybe it's all a dream. Or maybe it's only the catch-end of a dream gaze gone bad . . .' and the Hayward clown was saying:

'Never mind, Nigel. Try not to speculate too much about it. A lot has to come out in the wash . . . Fay, did you speak to Dulton?'

But when he went over to where she was standing on the front steps beside the big plaster urns full of daisies and stinging-nettles, she had gone. She was upstairs leaning against one of the cottage windows of a ward, her long chestnut hair shifting beside the red gladioli someone was arranging in a vase. Then Hayward's buzzer went. There was a patient to be admitted, and a psychopath on a court order asking for his discharge, and three women had beaten up one of the outside workers in the laundry. When he came back, Miss Fletton was helping three old ladies into her car for a spin and a hair-do for tonight.

'Fay, did you see Ken Dulton?' But they were waving back at him and smiling as they turned into the drive, and the quivering arrow of hot sound came again from the amplifiers in the trees and shot the birds with a clap out of their dark tree holes:

'I Hope I Hope I Hope It's Me'.

It was time for him to go and do out-patient ECT.

On Tuesdays they put screens across the lofty recreation hall with faded crêpe Christmas chains and bells still swinging from its rafters, and rows of chairs with a supermarket wire basket beside each for the patient to put his shoes and belt and rings and bags and teeth in. Then they were called one by one from behind the screen:

'Hullo, Mr Weekes. How are you this week? Do you still have the same feeling of worthlessness? Taking your tablets all right? . . . Hullo, Mrs Hull. How is she today? Has she cooperated at all in the house this week? Has she spoken at all? Good afternoon, Mr Lapp. How's your head this week? Does it feel your own yet? Do you still think it's been taken over by someone else?' There was never time to ask more than this, and by the time the patient had given his simple reply, the Sister was standing there with the needle and the patient was counting and he was out and the electric tiara was on his temples. His toes turned up in his stockinged feet like a baby's. Then he lay still and was wheeled away. Half an hour later he would be sitting up on the bed drinking tea and asking:

'Have I had the treatment yet?' An hour later he would be in the hospital bus going home, while Hayward with his kindly performer's voice would be asking the last patient:

'You see, unless I know what drugs you're on, I don't know what kind of an anaesthetic to give you.'

'The tablets are black and green I think' the slow slurred voice replied. 'But I can't remember the name. My memory's not what it was.'

'Never mind. It happens to all of us. Just let me have your own doctor's name and we'll get on to him on the blower.'

'I'm sorry. I ought to know. But my memory's shocking these days.'

'Not to worry. We all have our lapses. Where does he live?'

The patient sat there shaking her head and apologizing. Her stockings were down. Her roll-on was in the basket under the bed with her shoes and bag. The needle and the black case were ready.

'I'm sorry,' she tried to beat her head only the drugs had taken her drive away. Hayward's buzzer went again. It was the Mental Welfare Officer. The Miss Dennys wanted to see him again and the Welfare Officer wasn't happy about Mrs Bassey and thought she ought to be brought into hospital under Section 25.

'Right. I'll go and see her. See them all. When I've finished this clinic.'

The Miss Dennys lived on the Bendy Lane Estate. The fields seemed to hum with green as Hayward set out. The sandy red banks of the river had heaped up over the centuries into red-stone walls and red-brick barns and red farms with huge staring windows as arrogant and proprietary as the farmers' wives who met him on their drives:

'Do I know you, Dr Hayward? Ought I to know you? Is your family from this part of the world? You aren't one of the Civil War Haywards?'

The Miss Dennys had been farm servants till they grew too old for heavy work and had moved into one room in an old timber and thatch cottage clayed on to the old city wall by the Abbey. But Cross Friary in the Parish of St James had been needed for the ladies' toilet and the cigarette advertisement so the two old ladies had been decanted to the Bendy Lane Estate. The younger one was waiting for him on the landing with her ingratiating smile:

'All we want is to get back into Severnbridge. We liked Severnbridge, and we don't know anyone here.' Hayward could hear the shouts of the older Miss Denny echoing round the empty four-bedroomed flat they had been given. They had been servants all their life and had no furniture except the parting gifts of their mistress, a walnut veneered sideboard lined with velvet and two deckchairs. The elder Miss Denny had complained of worms in her head ever since the move.

'If only you could get us back to Severnbridge' the younger sister giggled and touched Hayward's wrist. The Abbey had been left and the shire hall scrubbed and refaced and railed round from the traffic. They looked like something from a child's Toy-Town cut-out set; two glossy dummies in a cage beside the girl's thighs advertising cigarettes. Hayward made out another prescription for Miss Denny's head and promised to get in touch with the housing department and take them for a drive one day. Then he went on to Hewitts where Mr and Mrs Bassey lived.

The thick teak gates at the bottom of the drive were wider and taller than their chalet home itself. A studded leather dog's collar was fixed across them and a 'Keep Off' notice nailed beside it: 'Alsatians patrolling. This means you.' In the bungalow window behind stood a gin bottle in a white crochet-work basket. Mr Bassey came to the door and offered Hayward a drink. He was about forty with receding ginger hair. He dressed immaculately in a starched white shirt and a blazer with a crest on the pocket. She'd been a kid during the war and lost everything, he explained. 'I think that upset her. That's the cause of it all. And her father was in the death camps. That's enough to set anyone off, isn't it?' His Adam's apple moved up and down. Hayward looked at his blazer badge:

'Were you in the RAF?' Mr Bassey shook his head. He hadn't been passed as fit for military service. He'd had a bad chest and gone into the Parks and Gardens Department of the local borough. He filled a glass with water and opened a Nembutal capsule and sprinkled it on and took it through to his wife. She was sitting up in their big satin-upholstered bed biting the inside of her cheek. Her cheek-bones stuck out under her eyes. Her collar-bone bulged through her nightdress. There were grains of Nembutal scum round her mouth when she had swallowed her husband's draught. Mr Bassey sat down and waited.

'Do you mind if we talk alone?'

'Her father was in the camps.'

'I see.'

'People say, don't they Doreen, that I've got a private army down there' he pointed over the fields towards the Bendy Lane Estate. 'A private army to topple the state over when I couldn't even get a bit of my own private property down' he laughed and slapped his pigskin gloves against his grey-flannel trousers. 'I think they say it to frighten Doreen. They know her father was in the camps.'

'I see. Do you mind if I have a word with her alone?' Mr Bassey said nothing but he lifted his gloves off his knee and got up.

'I'll be down the garden at the cages if you want me,'

'Does your husband still work in the Parks and Gardens Department?'

'No' Mrs Bassey said softly. Her throat heaved when she spoke as though every word hurt her. 'He breeds the pups.'

'The Alsatians?' She nodded. 'What for?'

'It's a popular man's dog now. And he's a certificated bailiff so he needs them. He never cared much working in the parks. Even when the council issued gloves for cleaning round the bushes, and got showers fitted, it was nasty work and he got bad dreams from what was behind those bushes. He used to come home and have another bath then clean out the fridge and throw away anything left over from yesterday. He couldn't stand the cheese near the sausage, or anything shut up. Even the beds had to be kept open all day. He used to think the sheets would fester if there wasn't a through draught. And he'd get up in the night and have another bath and wipe the water off the window-sills in case that festered too. They tried him in the Japanese Gardens, but people were just as filthy there he said. What he really liked doing was crazy-paving and laying grass. And trimming and pruning. And demolishing. So when he'd saved a bit of money of his own he got himself this bulldozer-thing, and then I think he was really happy. He's always been a careful punctual man, and if he said he'd be along at nine to have the old tree down or the coach-house or the old cottage, along he'd be. And he'd come home different – not moithered any more if you see what I mean. Instead of going straight to the bath or coming up to me and whispering: "Something rotting in that fridge. Something festering on that wall . . . By-the-by, Doreen, did you wash your hands after you paid your 'brief respects' just now in the Taj Mahal?" he'd get out the car and we'd go for a drive.

'"They'll fine you I expect" he would warn his client when we went out to see some chap who wanted something brought down. "Fifty or a hundred quid for knocking down your old squint-eyed château. Do you mind?" And then one day he saw this old house with a black thatch full of dead birds, and he wasn't happy till that came down. "Filthy spider's web" he would say when we went past. We'd never lived in a second-hand home. The thought upset him. He got bad dreams again and went to the dentist and had all his teeth out. But those thatched cottages in Severnbridge still upset him. "This is a great historic city" he would say, "and we want to keep it that way." Then he'd put rubber gloves on and tip caustic soda down the drain. "I don't like to think what the pipes are like in those Cross Friars crotchy old properties. Fungus. Cancer. It will all spread and spread, that thatch, till we're back in the world of apes again." There was a bad fire here in the seventeenth century I think it was, and these cottages had somehow survived. He started reading about this fire. Everything he could lay his hands on. "The Great Fire of Severnbridge" – he used to talk about nothing else. You could almost see the flames coming out of his own mouth when he said it: "Huh. Huh! Doreen, did you happen to notice if Rodney washed his hands after that toilet visit just now? I know he had a brief 'hallo' in the Taj just now. I saw him." Then he helped run a club for these kids, and they helped him with the dogs. They still do. They're out there now I think. They said the old ladies in Cross Friars were careless with the heaters, that's what caused the fire. You should hear him going on about the thatch. "It's so dirty" he says, "and full of mice and birds." You'd think the niggers were after him the way he goes on about it.'

Just then Mr Bassey came back. He'd got his yellow pigskin gloves on and was carrying a pigskin brief-case:

'Duty calls' he said. 'I've done my check on the dogs. We keep the dogs because Doreen gets scared. Her father was in the camps as I told you, and she gets nervy at night. Well I must be off, doctor. My small organization is running a holiday scheme for autistic children with ice-cream and the lot. And incidentally, Doreen, you can count me out of any Christmas fun you may be plotting up for us this year because I'm organizing Christmas cheer for the old people. I shall be on duty throughout the festive season carrying good fayre and seasonal chicken and pud round to folks worse off than ourselves . . . She represses it all, doctor. She represses the camps' he said as they went down the drive. 'I think she may do herself some harm if we don't get her into treatment by hook-or-by-crook.' The boys were sitting in Mr Bassey's car. They went off together.

'Do you think we ought to have her in for observation?' the Medical Welfare Officer was sitting in his car waiting for Hayward, arranging the things on the shelf under his steering wheel into three neat piles: metal, paper and cloth, the categories seemed to be.

'No. Him.'

The Welfare Officer burst out laughing: 'I see. Just as he's about to be given the freedom of the city, we whip him away to Gledhull under Section 25.'

'Why is he to be given the freedom of the city?'

'They wouldn't get far with their clearance and replanning programmes without him. He demolishes. He prevents squatters and hippies from moving into old houses waiting for the axe and sterilizing the land. There was a group – a sort of commune – moved into Cross Friars not long ago, and the Planning Committee were in a tizzy because the houses were to come down in a few years. But Mr Bassey got them out.'

'How?'

'I dunno. The City Council kept pretty quiet. They never put contracts into writing when it's a case of wrecking or demolishing.'

'How did he get the Miss Dennys out?'

'The two old sisters on the Bendy Lane Estate? Well, it was one of those old timber and thatch cottages and there was no proper facilities. It was a slum. Well, so there's no action to be taken about Mrs Bassey?'

'No. I don't think so. Not unless we can get him in.' The Welfare Officer's laughter was still in Hayward's ears as he passed Cross Friars, Parish of St James. The few remaining buildings stood like ventriloquists' dummies behind the traffic railings. The people of Severnbridge had voted for roads and hypermarkets and against homes and free public transport. The long-stay wards at Gledhull had always had mattresses on the corridors and eating places between the beds, but people voted as though they thought of *themselves* as the long-stay patients. Miss Fletton was always trying to get Severnbridge to visit Gledhull. Instead it seemed to Hayward as he drove through the city, that Gledhull had taken over there.

The green hummed in the fields and hills as he went back to the hospital. Green swelled in the hedges and broke from the beaks of birds and burst from walls and gutters and thatches; the great clots of green that had seemed mysterious and half-threatening this morning were merely mocking now. A booby green, mobbing him as he drove along. Jokers bleeding to death, and clowns on the fields. He went straight to Miss Fletton's room when he got back and she was there.

'Fay, did you have it out with Dr Dulton about Jean Gold? What about Hennock's date down here? Is he really going to try it on?'

Miss Fletton was leaning over her neat legs painting her toenails and stroking the chamois bows that made up the tops of her sandals with a child's toothbrush.

'Cheer up, Alex.' She was sniffing slightly as she bent over. 'Cheer up, Alex. Gledhull will soon be down,' she spoke through her nose and at her feet and the floor. 'It'll soon be turned over to the hard-garment industry as I always said it should. The oldsters will all have died off, and the young ones will be repatriated back to the community. The patient's place is in the home' she said, dreamily re-bunching the bows across her toes.

'What a hideous idea! Their homes are the last places I'd like to treat my patients in. Di's mother fixed that lobotomy out of revenge. And when Miss Gold's mother came down last time she brought her daughter see-through undies and a wig. Families are more destructive than hospitals.'

'Well, let's say then that the patient's place is back in the community.'

'Back on the Bendy Lane Estate with one shop and one bus an hour to the city centre four miles away, and knowing all the time that Claypits and St James went to make way for an advertisement for cigarettes, and that the city centres are too good for *you*. *That* community is an institutionalized invalid already. Yes, I suppose it's safe to pull the asylums down now. Now that there are all these higher drugs and advanced branches of surgery and clearance, and manipulation.'

'Now don't you hold me responsible for the Bendy Lane Estate. The trouble with you Alex is that you are one-hundred-per-cent feeling. What branch of medicine would you *really* like to be in? Ken Dulton asked me at lunch, but I couldn't honestly say.'

'So you did see him about this latest bit of slum-clearance?'

Fay kicked the record-player on with her toes. She had instructed her assistants to buy French bread and beer and salami, and to stay away from their office for at least two hours. Then she had laid the table and waited for Dulton.

'Four leucs! Four fees!' she pushed her chin out at him when he came dancing in. 'The surgeon won't come for less than a quartet. That's why Di and Pauline were done. But you're not going to try it again on Miss Gold, are you, Ken? Miss Gold's just institutionalized. Her only other trouble is that she's anti-male and there I thoroughly sympathize. She should be discharged to a women's lib group with plenty of psychodrama to get it all out of her.' Fay opened the beer and they sat down to their working lunch. She meant first of all to tick the Consultant off about his flippant attitude to social case work and getting his patients community-oriented, and only later to bring up the subject of the surgeon's date down here. But Dulton took a large bite out of his French bread and a sip of beer and tipped his chair back and grinned and forestalled her:

'Fay' he munched happily, wrapping his fingers one by one round his dark crust of bread, and pretending to sigh, 'if only mankind hadn't got up off all fours.'

'You'd be pretty uninfectious Ken, pardon my saying so, if you hadn't never got up off them four plates of meat.'

'I was thinking more of you than of me,' he grinned back innocently picking with his strong separate fingers at some surplus meat and prising two slices of it apart with his hard red tongue as he chewed. He'd take her out for a drive after this evening's do, and give her a meal somewhere smart and then take her home and screw her. His hands shook slightly as he lifted his beer. He pushed his glass back and opened his lips slightly and ran one finger down her wrist. 'Miss Crowe's been admitted again. Ugh! Poor Hayward. How I used to hate examining old ladies. Their breasts are so clammy to touch – like raw lamb's liver – Have you got nice little gay lemon-shaped breasts?' His face ripened shyly. 'Fay, come and play with me,' he screwed his face up and grinned. His glasses misted over. He took them off, but the skin round his eyes was mauve and tracked with pimples.

'You look better with them on.' He grinned sheepishly and dropped them back on.

'Fay,' he put his hand on her knee, 'I want those pants down and that bra off and those breasts liberated.'

'What a rush-job you medics are,' she dropped her hands limply down beside her doeskin bag. 'Could we get down to business, Ken?'

'Yes, if only women hadn't taken to getting up off all fours and hiding their genitalia! Fay, in the MO's room we can never decide whether this girlie footwork and your polka-dotted tits are meant to tell us that you are an easy lay or a hard one. Still, it adds up to the same thing, doesn't it?' He was surprised to see her stiffen. 'So I want those pants off and those breasts as free as birds. How easily your nipples come!' Fay's grin was back on her face, but her neck was red and there was sweat beside her nose as she folded her arms and said with a kind of croak:

'And me a parson's daughter and all! But I'd take on ten of you, Ken, and make you turn over in your graves.' Her grin was frightened though, and hideous, but he didn't see what it meant and went on:

'So there's no need to bring out the high-minded artillery any more, or the heavy sociology plant, because we've taken the point. I'm going to have you somewhere tonight.'

She yawned. 'Thanks, but fat and forty doesn't interest me all that much.' But her foot was moving up and down very quickly under the chair as she spoke and sweat stood on her forehead and in her hair. 'The older medics round here don't seem to have read a book or netted in an idea since they qualified. Driven any good cars lately?' she jerked her face out at Dulton and they both sat there stiffly, both flushed, both hurt, but neither daring to make the next move or discover exactly how far they were wounded. Then Fay began:

'I see now why you're so keen to experiment on Miss Gold. Men never feel safe with women until they've reduced them to flesh and things. So many Paulines. So many Di's with their legs apart waiting. That's how you like your women – willing vessels for anything. Then you feel safe and good. And they are so conniving and so forgiving afterwards! You'd never get a man to be your willing victim. And other men wouldn't stand for it either.' The last words came out as a scream. But the scream became a laugh and Dulton joined in. 'A thing!' Fay poured beer on his hair and he laughed sheepishly as he watched it drip down through his fingers, still not knowing whether it were war or play. He had planned such a happy evening for himself while his wife and family were away, and Fay had won each round of her daily battle against bureaucracy and inhumanity with her woman's commonsense and moral nerve till now when she suddenly saw herself as the doctors saw her: a mere hysteric they tried to placate; an ageing virgin they felt sorry for, making her last bid. They sat there in silence while beer dripped off the table, both waiting for the other to make the first move and indicate whether it was war or play. Then they carefully extricated themselves.

'Incidentally' Miss Fletton began in a hard amiable voice, 'talking of hysteria, Alex Hayward's been having kittens about Miss Gold and Hennock's date down here. When's it fixed for? Alex got in quite a tizzy. Soon he'll be talking about his Good Gates and his Bad Ones.' They laughed, slightly but together. The breach began to close. 'So do you really think it would help her?'

'It was just an idea, that's all.' Dulton always liked to get his patients' consent for brain-surgery, and he wasn't even all that certain that it would be appropriate in this particular case. The patient didn't want it and would never forgive him and it would go bad on him. He already had two millstones round his neck every time he went on that ward.

But Fay's accusation about his motives had upset him, and the only way he could prove their integrity was to carry the business right through. He wasn't a sadist. He was a scientist and a healer. And Fay too, he noticed, suddenly seemed less anxious to pursue her traditional crusader's role. She hadn't apologized, but her silence was the expression of apology, or concession, and having the initiative suddenly allowed Dulton's anger to grow. She had roused him and then rebuffed him. His appetite grew as well.

'Last time I let you sit in on a pre-frontal assault' he said, 'you passed out.'

'True. I was out for the count,' she dropped her soft chamois hands beside her doeskin bag and leaned over and spoke as though she had a cold in her nose, 'oud for the coud.'

'It is rather grisly and traumatic the first time round' Dulton smiled. 'Perhaps you'd better try again. Hennock will probably use a "local", and there are some pretty interesting data sometimes when you pass an electric current over the speech and visual centres.'

'But will it be gory, Ken?'

'Not with this new laser method. Catch!' Dulton tossed his journal over. 'You can do your homework first. And now I must be off. Bye-bye Fay, and thanks for the nice lunch.'

'Bye Ken,' she flapped her hand at him and repeated in a small nasal voice: 'dice dunch.'

'Any chance of seeing you tonight after the fancy-dress?' he swung back casually on the door-knob. For a moment they looked at each other dispassionately, then Fay took out her eyelash mirror and tested her upper lids:

'Bay-be.' She sat down when Dulton had gone and held her handkerchief at her nostrils and cried silently. She had told her assistants to stay away on conferences, case-reviews, 'caesarian sections, or whatever you like'. She had told them to clear the room first though, but they had not, and it was littered with the things she had trained them to have – lip-mirrors still propped against the filed case-histories, gloves for handling nylons pinned by tiny pink-and-chocolate pegs from the desk lamps, and everywhere silver sandals, atomizers, discarded swabs, washed eyelashes and abandoned fingernails. When Hayward came in, she was throwing them about:

'You and your Things!' she shouted at him, cursing.

'Oh my word!' the Sister stood in the day-room of Sixteens, 'you are all busy in here. What are you making, Miss Gold?' Miss Gold, usually so uncooperative, was tearing sheets of coloured paper up and folding them roughly into hats and caps and aprons and skirts and dropping them on to the floor. 'Is this your mother's address dear?' she whispered to her. 'Is she your closest relative? Your next-of-kin?' Miss Gold stepped back with chemical green paper against her grey face. The Sister stepped back with her: 'What are you making for *me* to wear tonight, eh? Tell us. There's a dear! We're going to have such a lovely evening, aren't we? You won't get out of there you know. You know you won't, don't you? Come and sit in the office with me while I get my bits and bobs together and tell me all about it.'

The phone went and the Sister disappeared into the office and came out again smiling:

'That was your mother, dear. She's glad they're going to balance you up again and get you right. She sends her love and asks me to tell you that the hairdresser she works for is going to give you a free hairdo and a facial afterwards. I expect your mother's really looking forward to having you home again when the grey matter's been sorted out, and getting you back into circulation. My daughter says there are some nice little jobs going in the new Ministry that's moved down to this part of the world. Jean . . .' Miss Gold stood there bent forwards with her hands crossed over her genitals. 'Jean my duck, you'll feel ever so much better afterwards. Jean, if you don't sign, they'll do it over your head . . . Put you under a section and then where will you be? Jean, please, we're going to have a lovely party tonight, and my daughter's waiting for me at the end of the lane. She wants me to help her match some of those new sling-back shoes for her annual leave, and I don't want to disappoint her. Do you fancy a pair? In mole or lemon? When you're well again we could go out together on the razzle eh, and buy you a pair. So be a good girl,' the Sister stooped down and looked up into Jean's face and tried to make her smile. Then she cleared the hair-dryer off a chair and carried the chair out to the tea tables on the corridor where a few patients still sat over their chopped sausage and chips and little pink and yellow cupcakes. Hot yellow custard steamed up from them, sprinkled with hundreds and thousands. The Sister placed the chair at the cakes and tried to make Jean sit down at them, at the same time calling: 'There's a dear! Tell me all about it,' and 'Someone! Relief! I'm supposed to be off duty and there's no one to relieve me . . . So what are you going to wear, Jean? Tell us. Let us into the secret? Relief! Someone . . .'

The Sister went back into her office and sat at her desk trying to write up the ward report with a blunt pencil and at the same time find something to sharpen it with and see what was wrong with the hair-dryer and slip the little coloured cakes into her shopping bag and stare down the hospital lane to see if she could see her daughter.

'Someone! Relief! Jean, they have them in midnight and albatross as well, the sling-back shoes. Someone!'

Dr Dulton stood there. 'All right, Sister. You can take yourself off' he smiled. 'I've got my keys, and I'd like to have a chat with Miss Gold.' He made a pot of coffee on the ring beside the gas-fire and laid out two cups and invited Jean in.

By six o'clock almost all the patients were out on the lawns. The nurses had launched coloured-paper streamers and bows up the walls and into the trees. The fairy-lights were on, and music came out of the amplifier by the chapel:

'Rainy Days Don't Worry Me,
There's a Rainbow that I Can See . . .'

A group of women with a nurse were watching a puppet show. Some boys were fishing for ducks at another booth. There was a trampoline. There was a display by local girl gymnasts; some Rotarians in blazers were playing 'It's a Hap-Hap-Happy Day' on jerky erratic handbells. At the edge of the fair there was an aquarium. The patients stood round watching the fat fish hanging peacefully in the water.

'It's not really an aquarium' the owner confided to Hayward. 'It's a fish farm.' He spread a tablecloth over his stall and thrust out a bundle of filthy leaflets. 'Ladies and gentlemen . . . here is the answer to our river-pollution problem. You know what the rivers are like round here. Filth,' he held up a ball of detergent froth like candy-floss. 'Feel! You're not married are you, so why are you having a good feel?' he asked Di. She giggled. 'In ten years' time there'll be no more fish in the rivers. They'll all be in tanks like this. Adaptation. That's the law of survival.' Di and Pauline wandered on. No fish in the rivers. No birds in the sky. No people on the streets. 'You can adapt yourself to almost anything, they say.' Hayward got out his car. He would take Miss Gold away.

Patients at Gledhull were interviewed weekly for the first month after their admission, then monthly, then yearly.

Jean Gold had been admitted two years before Hayward came to the hospital. She had assaulted her mother, a widow, and had been brought in as a voluntary patient:

'She's always trying to read my thoughts' she had complained.

'She tried to get inside my head.' The houseman had written this down and asked her about her sex-life, masturbation, drugs, etc. Then he had leaned over and asked softly:

'Do you ever have thoughts . . . Do you ever want to . . . do anything?' She hadn't replied. He had shut up her case-book and smiled again: 'Well now, I have to take this away.' He had taken the history to Dr Dulton who was sitting at the round table under the electric light in the MO's room. Dulton had read the report and written underneath 'paranoid schizophrenia . . . ECT . . . Insulin . . . Tophranil . . . Imipramine?' then handed the book back. When Hayward looked at the book four years later he found only reports on her fits of anger, reports on various EEGs, her responses to shock treatment and the various drugs they had tried. It was always hard to find a room free to talk to patients in. There was the Sister's office, but after a few minutes the phone would go and the Sister would come in to answer it, or the door-knob would rotate slowly backwards and forwards and a nurse or a patient would be standing there waiting to catch the doctor as he came out. Now for the first time the ward was empty and quiet. The music struck up outside. The patients were all out there shaking hands with the Bishop and the Mayor and queueing for gifts from a bran-tub organized by a priest in a food-stained cassock and sash. For the first time, Hayward had privacy with his patient:

'Jean, shall I take you away?' He knew nothing about her really except for these treatment reports and an account of an interview with her mother:

'She was a lovely child . . . No trouble at all. But just when she should have started getting interested in boys and having a good time, she let herself go and lost interest in life. I did my best. Took her out. Took her dancing. Had her weight seen to. Took her to a specialist about her periods. Got her thoroughly examined. Invited people in. Took her to Paris. But no. That wasn't good enough for her. Then some young people came to the flat next door. So I went over and explained how it was to them. Told them that she didn't get out enough. Didn't get enough fun. They promised to give me a hand with her. Then Jean just let herself go. "My affairs are quite under control" she shouted at me and tore all her clothes off her and put them on the gas stove with all the burners lit and stood there naked . . . you know . . . you know what she was doing . . . It was then she got a milk bottle and broke it over my head . . .'

Jean stood there by the window in a paper crown and paper skirt she had made. Below, the patients in their costumes were being knit into a long chain by the social workers, one in front of the other, hands on the hips of the one in front. 'Horsie Horsie Don't You Stop' the music started. The long human caterpillar shuffled across the lawns in front of the fancy-dress judges: 'Just Let Your Feet Go Clippety-Clop.'

'Jean, shall I take you away? I think I could get you some proper psychiatric help. I'm having a partial analysis as part of my training and the Institute where I go is often willing to take disturbed people like you for a very small fee. I'm not earning much, but my sister might be willing to look after you, and later we could find you a job . . .'

'It would be very noisy though' she replied. She lifted one leg and stood there poised. He watched her.

'Yes, I see. After four years in an institution, choices are very hard to take for yourself. Even I feel that sometimes.'

'And I get such a poor night's sleep even here with my nightly tipple.'

'I'd see to that. And later on you'd be able to get a job. You were a secretary weren't you, before?'

'Yes, but they do everything on dictaphones and tapes these days.'

'Still, once you'd got your shorthand speeds back . . .'

'But you must have a good salary' she frowned and blurted out almost angrily, 'in a high-up job like this.'

'I'm only a student, Jean. I earn less than some of the nurses here and even that is docked for food and a room next to a refractory ward where the patients prevent me from getting a bit of sleep when I've been up all night.' But she wasn't interested in his room or the meals he took at week-ends at the far corner of the overcrowded long-stay ward while at the other end the women he distinguished from patients only by their white overalls formed the old men into long lines for food, toiletting, washroom, food, toiletting, and more food from hot metal food cars full of steaming bruised potatoes with pilchard laid on top.

'Will you come with me?'

'Isn't Dr Dulton coming back to see me?'

'Has he been to see you? When?'

'He came this evening with another high-up specialist who is interested in my case. He *is* my doctor after all' she frowned and reproached him.

'And what did they say?'

'I'd rather discuss that with him when he comes back.' They both stared down at the party below. Dulton stood in a chef's apron and cap by the ox-roast waiting to carve.

'I'll take you away before the party is over. I'll find you a reputable therapist. An anti-psychiatrist, if you know what I mean. I've rung my sister incidentally, and she says . . .'

'But people are so noisy these days. So inconsiderate and dirty. So I do and I don't.'

'Don't what?'

The dark elms along their frontier brought the first drifts of night. Jean stared out, then opened her big handbag very slowly. He saw they had drugged her quite recently. Her voice was slurred. She opened and shut her mouth to try and get some saliva to speak: 'It's all very complicated,' she gazed out at the elms. 'I don't want people to read anything into this.'

'Into what?'

'You and me. You see Dr Dulton is like a father to me. He understands my peculiar personality and – my gifts.' She slowly opened her bag again. 'He knows my individual set-up.' She stood there with her mouth open trying to get enough saliva to explain: 'I've got a date with Dr D. Dr D.'s the man for me.' Hayward pictured Dulton sitting there with his strong smooth hands; dark, authoritative, charismatic; leaning back as Jean talked, nodding, listening attentively, head held back, eyes shut:

'Go on. Let it come. Can you remember anything before that, Jean? Your father, what was *he* like? How did he die? Did he touch you, tickle you, as fathers sometimes do with their small daughters?'

She shook her head and thought. 'I was six when he died. He was very small, much smaller than my mother, and he always said if there were another world war, he would kill us all. We were standing alone in a field by some bushes and an aeroplane was being towed past on the back of a lorry. And the hawthorn was blackened. The foxgloves were all blackened and scorched as though the sun had come down with black rays, instead of white.'

Dulton had looked at her and nodded, 'Try to go on. What do you associate with those black rays? Have a fag, and take your time.'

'It was my birthday, and they gave me some doll's clothes and let me chime the clock and invite a friend to tea. But my father bit a piece out of the side of his glass and the friend was sent away, and my parents' bed was empty next day. Smooth and flat and cold. And the woman next door put her face through a hole in the fence and I could see the wart on her lip moving in the hole, and she put her hand over the fence and lifted me over and gave me a doll as big as myself. Its arms kept flopping on to me and I hid it behind a bush and when I went back to see if it was safe, my father was lying there with a gramophone. He was lying on his side with his back to me and the gramophone was playing:

'Ninety-nine out of a hundred want to be killed.'

'Kissed or killed, Jean?'

'And the man turned round and it wasn't my father.'

'What did he look like?'

'He looked like my father.'

'And what did he do to you?' But she could only remember a hot crackling macintosh, a hot tarred road, and the black hot tentacles of the sun shrivelling the flowers on the bushes and making them sicken and steam.

'Do you think your father touched you that day? . . .' Dulton had put his head on one side. 'Mmm?' he smiled shyly at her. 'Mmm?' he asked gently and patiently. 'Mmm?' he gave her all the time and attentiveness that there was. 'Do you think your father *did* anything to you that hot day?' But she could only remember that the lilac screwed itself up thin and black. Dulton looked at her and nodded 'Mmm?' again, his head still tilted slightly. Then he looked surreptitiously at the watch strapped on the inside of his wrist and took the Biro from his breast-pocket and wrote one word on her case-notes. One fine Biro-stroke on the page, then he closed the book and put his Biro back. There were black Biro strokes above his white coat pocket:

'I think we're beginning to get somewhere at last, Jean. But I think that for the moment, until you're less sensitized, until we've got your hyper-reactivity reduced to manageable levels, we should leave it there. This little bit of engineering might help us to help you walk slowly through that childhood experience again. It's such a tiny and subtle bit of – of elision – that we would probably only use a 'local' so it wouldn't be all that different from the time you had those stitches put in yout hand. OK?' He put his head slightly to one side and looked at her again and gave her all the time he had, all the time there was, all the space round. 'We wouldn't bother about refined and expensive techniques like this unless we thought you were a person with a strong texture and a firm hold on your imaginative experience and the ability to go through the complete complex.'

'Will you come with me then, Jean?' Dr Hayward took his keys out. But she stood there with her *presque vue*.

'Dr Dulton has started to untangle me at last' she said in a soft hoarse voice. 'I think we've almost got there.' Outside the music started up and they were dancing.

'Jean please come with me while they're all out there.' He took her hand. She withdrew it sharply.

'How rough your hands are! Like a cactus. Like a prickly pear. Dr Dulton's are rather smooth and soft. Like petals. We had a long talk and he's beginning to untangle me . . . ' The blackened hawthorn; the sickened lilac; the tinkling gramophone, all three coming from behind the man's back; the man turning; was it your father? Do you think he touched you? Did he suddenly stand up? . . . Hayward looked at the case-notes lying on the Sister's desk. The one word the consultant had written down was 'florid'; stuck in the pocket at the back of the folder was the surgeon's form, and Jean had signed it. Tomorrow she would be drugged and put to bed till medical examinations, physical measurements, intelligence tests and personality assessments had been taken, filed and programmed.

Then they would shave her head. Hayward could see her standing there leaning forward while her cable of brown hair fell to the floor. When she saw, she would cross her hands over her stomach and want to change her mind.

'Never mind, Jean. It will grow again' Dulton would reassure her. 'Sister, have you got a bit of tissue paper and a box? We'll look after it carefully Jean, I assure you. We'll keep it safe till the awkward corners have been rubbed off.' He was wrapping the warm brown hair up with his small carnivore fingers.

'No please. I'm sorry, but I'm afraid I've changed my mind after all. I'm sorry to be such an awkward customer' she was laughing huskily, then bending over. 'Very well Doctor. Very good. Yes, that's comfortable. Lovely. Right. Lovely. Love-ly' the voice growing more drowsy and institutionalized. 'Very good. You must know, Doctor.'

'Jean, will you come? Please! Now.' But she stood very upright and walked away from Hayward in her paper skirt and crown like a queen to the fire-escape door and banged on it till a nurse came up and let her out and down the steps to the dance. On the way she passed a stall of streamers and took one pink roll circuitously round to where Dr Dulton stood carving the roast and unfurled it at him. It touched his shoulder. He turned and smiled:

'Right. Will you have this next dance with me, Jean?'

'Get Off My Cloud' the singer's voice huffed saucily out off the chapel wall. Jean and Dulton were dancing together like conspirators and laughing at Hayward up there. King and Queen, Man and Woman, in a conspiracy he didn't understand. He had only been at Gledhull two years. She had been there for four, waiting for the Consultant to come.

'One Paddle Two Paddle' the music came again. The nurses began to dance with the patients. More and more of them were drawn into the dance in the republic of the meek. Jean was still dancing with the Consultant. She would win first prize as his bride. Hayward ran down the fire-escape. In the crowd he lost sight of Dulton and Jean Gold.

'Excuse me, Doctor,' a man tapped his arm, 'you won't remember me but I was the Terror of Tens' he winked. 'Five times they "did" me till they got me right . . . I'm right as rain now and I work in the supermarket down the road, and when that's closed there's always a jumble-sale to go to where they give you tea and a fag maybe. The tricks I got up to' he grinned and touched his head. 'Soon they say there won't be a hospital here at all, because you'll have put all that grey matter right, eh? You can still see my scars, look!' he pulled at a soft down of reddish hair that was beginning to haze over his recently shaved scalp. 'Do they provide the wigs on the National Health when you've had the "op"?'

Hayward excused himself and pushed on. Beyond the booths and the lawn laid out for dancing the grass stood rough and defiant in prickly stubble. The birds were beginning to creep heavily over it, round and round then launching themselves over the hay-bales to the brims of the hedges. A flat veil of mist hung beyond, then the black portcullis of the elms that were their frontier, then the first lights of Severnbridge.

It seemed to come nearer and nearer each week, the silver and blue dish of its motorway signs hung in the air suddenly with the words 'Gledhull' written up as prominently as Newcastle or Cardiff.

'Mind you' the ex-patient was saying, following him along, 'the doctors still take a great interest in my case. And they let me come to all the socials and bingo's. I won a quarter of tea again last week. Mind you, I've had my downfalls, many of them, but the doctors and nurses here have never let me down.' Night slumped down suddenly between the arms of the trees. The city clicked up another pan of lights. 'It may seem a bit of a downfall at the time, but in the long run it's the whole community benefits' the man went on, 'and they say, they do say, you can live without almost anything these days. Your liver, your kidney, even your heart, eh?' he ran his fingers through his downy juvenile new hair.

Hayward would get in touch with the press and publicize the recent advances in neuro-surgery. But his voice sounded infantile and unconvincing as he pushed his way calling to Dr Dulton through the crowd. His anger he saw had been institutionalized and put to bed, and Dulton and Jean Gold were still dancing. It wasn't rape after all. Human dignity was after all an adventitious thing, and it was a hospital wedding. The patients of Jean's ward were laughing and clapping as the Consultant paraded his bride down the passage they made – lining the route for the prize-winning couple's triumph.